K. M. PEYTON

Flambards in Summer

Illustrated by Victor G. Ambrus

OXFORD
UNIVERSITY PRESS

Oxford University Press, Great Clarendon Street, Oxford OX2 6DP

Oxford New York
Athens Auckland Bangkok Bogota Buenos Aires Calcutta
Cape Town Chennai Dar es Salaam Delhi Florence Hong Kong Istanbul
Karachi Kuala Lumpur Madrid Melbourne Mexico City Mumbai
Nairobi Paris Sao Paulo Singapore Taipei Tokyo Toronto Warsaw

and associated companies in
Berlin Ibadan

Oxford is a trade mark of Oxford University Press

British Library Cataloguing in Publication Data
Data available

Cover illustration by Angelo Rinaldi

ISBN 0 19 271781 2

Printed and bound in Great Britain by
Biddles Ltd, Guildford and King's Lynn

FOR
IRENE

Chapter 1

'A poor aviator lay dying
    At the end of a bright summer's day,
    His comrades were gathered around him
    To carry the fragments away.'

The R.F.C. ditty with the sad tune, which Christina had
sung several times with Will and his friends when he had been
home on leave, would not leave her head. They had all laughed
when they sang it, even the lines which went:

'Here's a health to the dead already,
    And hurrah for the next man who dies.'

When Will had been beside her, Christina had laughed, too. But when Will became 'the next man', the poor aviator in the song, she did not laugh any more. In fact, although she was only twenty-one, she did not think for some weeks that she would ever laugh again.

But in 1916 a young woman dressed in mourning did not evoke a second glance. There were too many of them. When she boarded the train with her luggage at Liverpool Street Station Christina decided that, as she was about to resume her life as if Will had never existed, she would discard her black as soon as she got to Flambards. 'You can't go round being a farmer in *black*,' she said to herself practically. 'It'll show every speck.' For a few minutes she felt very bold and calm. That was the way of it. She would be all right, she thought; she had got over it. But when the train was out in the country, and she saw the untouched hay-fields swinging in the soft August sunshine and the skylarks rising up over the thick dusty hedges with their ever-optimistic music, the awfulness came back, that Will had landed in a hay-field in France and lain in the grass and died of his wounds, while she had been at home peeling potatoes for Aunt Grace, who had been coming to lunch that day . . . it was a thought that still had the power to crush her into white, numb petrifaction. Thank God, she thought, pulling her eyes away from the window, she was not alone in the dingy carriage. The polite curiosity of the other occupants held her in check, her face composed. The smoke from the engine obscured the hay-fields. She was grateful.

She thought she had had no feelings at all about going back to Flambards. It was somewhere to go, no more. But as the train drew its smoky course across the Essex countryside she was less sure. She had wanted to go there to be alone. It was empty now, save for the two old servants, Mary and Fowler, and in its rambling wilderness she had supposed she would be able to find some sort of peace. She had loved it when she had lived there as a child, although it had never officially been her home, as it had Will's. Will had been born there; she, the orphan of the family, had merely been summoned there to live, whether she liked it or not. She had not been back since she and Will had run away together to get married, except once, fleetingly, for the funeral of Will's father. Now, officially, it belonged to Will's elder brother Mark, but in fact the old place was in limbo, belonging to a ghost, for no word had come from Mark since the fighting round Gaza in Palestine and he was posted as 'Missing'.

That was another thing that Christina did not want to think about. (There was, indeed, nothing left to think about that gave Christina any measure of happiness at all.)

'I must work,' she thought, 'and make myself very tired. And at Flambards there will be plenty of work to do.'

At least, if Flambards failed her, she would have the satisfaction of having tried.

When the train eventually came into the little home station, Christina remembered how she had felt before, returning to Flambards for old Russell's funeral, that it was like stepping back into another century. It was the same now, except that this time she was glad, not scornful. The porter was gathering his Darcy Pippins from the small orchard beyond the palings; he came hurrying, wiping his forehead under his cap. His dog lay panting in the shade, undisturbed by war or death, or even modern transport. Christina's luggage was bundled down, and several parcels besides, and a truck of heifers was uncoupled, and amongst the little, local commotion, Christina went out through the ticket-office and found Fowler waiting for her.

'Miss Christina, my dear!'

Christina had forgotten how old he was. He was as knotted as the porter's apple-trees, his cheeks red with old threaded veins, his hands trembling in his excitement. His eyes were full of tears, and Christina had to be brisk to stop the emotion overflowing, hers as well as his. It was not until she was up beside him in the wagonette and the horse was moving out into the dusty lane that she felt the imminent danger past.

'How is Flambards?' she said quickly, before he could ask after the painful subject of herself.

'The same, the same, miss—or ma'am, I should say. All falling to bits. It's patch this, patch that, inside and out, no end to it. And all makeshift, because Mr. Mark never left no money for it, and no instructions. Mary and I—well, it's been our life, the old place—we do our best, but we're past it now. We just try to keep it from getting too bad, for the time—' He faltered, unsure of how to finish. 'For whoever comes back, you understand.'

'Yes, I see.' Already, the conversation was back to the point Christina could never get away from.

'You've heard no news of Mr. Mark, ma'am?'

'No.'

'Will's death came as a terrible shock to us, Miss Christina. We both remember the boys being born here, you see. They're more to us than just employers. When you've been with a family all your life, you become a part of it yourself—without being disrespectful, ma'am.'

'Yes, of course.'

'And when we heard you were coming back, Mary and I— we—well, we were that excited—oh dear me! We laughed and cried in turns, wanting you to come back, you see, but not for the reason—the way it turned out, with Mr. Will being killed.'

'Yes.' Christina sat thinking, 'I shall have to go through all this again with Mary, but afterwards it will be all right.' She prayed that it would be all right. So far, her return was doing little to raise her spirits. Every turn in the lane and view across the fields was precisely as she had always remembered, but every view had been shared, before, with either Mark or Will. With Mark she had always been on horseback, with Will on foot, on the way to visit his dear friend Mr. Dermot, who had taught him to fly an aeroplane when he was just sixteen. Now, if she roamed these ways again, she would be alone.

'How are the horses?' she asked quickly, before Fowler could depress her any more. 'How many did you keep?'

'Why, miss, there's only old Pepper here, who we keep for the errands. All the hunters have gone. The Army took Treasure and Goldwillow, Drummer was sold after you went, and Wood-pigeon—the Army didn't want him on account of his legs not being all they should be—he was sold to a doctor to use in harness—'

'And Sweetbriar? Do you know what happened to her, after Mr. Dermot died?'

'No, ma'am, I never heard.'

Now Christina had to blow her nose, turning her head away. It was ludicrous that she had managed all right when the talk was of Will, but that she wept for the horses. 'It's a part of it all,' she thought desperately; she cried for everything that would never come back.

4

'Oh, yes, Miss Christina, you'll see big changes. All the best horses went into the Army and Mr. Lucas sold up the hounds—they were scattered around, a couple here and a couple there to whoever'ld take them. He went into the Army himself, in spite of his age, and got wounded about the same time as young Peter, his nephew. Not so badly, though. Young Peter's very bad, I hear.'

Christina shut her ears to the old man's narrative, letting his gentle voice get drowned in the dusty clip of the horse's hoofs and the distant clatter of the reapers over the fields. She felt she must protect herself somehow, get braced again for facing Flambards in all its solid reality, its dreadful emptiness. She knew perfectly well that when they turned in at the drive she would remember only the night Will had come for her in Mr. Dermot's Rolls-Royce and taken her to the Hunt Ball and asked her to marry him; she would remember nothing else. 'But I knew it would be like this,' she thought stubbornly. 'Afterwards it will be all right.'

These were the lanes she had ridden a thousand times with Mark. She shut her eyes for a bit, but the smell of dust and trampled grass and horse and leather was every bit as evocative. She set her teeth. 'Soon it will be all right.'

But however she had pictured Flambards in her mind, it did not measure up to Flambards in fact. When Pepper turned through the gates and into the drive, she realized immediately that Flambards in its present state offered precious little comfort. It had never been well cared for even before, but at least the paddocks had been grazed, the fences kept in order and the woods and coverts thinned and checked. Now, as the drive stretched ahead, the paddocks on the left-hand side were a jungle of shoulder-high grass with yellow ragwort flaring and thistledown floating in little clouds on the breeze. The same thistles coarsely sprouted up amongst the dried ruts of the once neatly gravelled drive, along with suckers and struggling saplings which had seeded from the woods that bordered the right-hand side. And as they drew nearer to the house Christina could scarcely make out the doors and windows for the rampant ivy. Beside the house the garden was now growing right up through the terrace, rough arms of flowering teasels rubbing against the terrace doors, the roses scarcely visible through the

suckers of wild plum and sloe that had been thrown out from the hedges. Only the big cedar-tree rose up, inviolate, out of the mess and, beyond the house, across the weedy expanse of dried mud that had once been the gravelled forecourt, the chestnuts soared in all their green, summer glory as Christina had always remembered, their spiked pale fruits ripening in great clusters against the sky.

Fowler brought Pepper to a halt in front of the house. Christina sat looking, not wanting to get down.

'Old Mary's a little deaf these days, ma'am. She won't have heard us. I'll get down and call her.'

'No,' Christina said quickly, 'don't.'

She looked at the house. It stared back, shrouded and empty. Not even the old foxhounds stirred on the doorstep. The house looked defeated beneath its strangling mantle, as if it would willingly disappear altogether. 'It feels like I do,' Christina thought.

'Drive on to the stables,' she said to Fowler. 'I would like to see them.'

The stables were worse. They, at least, had been neat and shining in the old days, as the house never had, but now the empty loose-boxes echoed to the solitary Pepper's hoofs as Fowler drew him up near the trough. A top-door swung disconsolately. Even the cats had gone, and grass grew between the cobbles. Fowler dropped his reins, and gave Christina a wry smile.

'A bit different, ma'am, from the old days?'

Christina felt her lips trembling. She sat up stiffly.

'We must have more than one horse, Fowler—a riding horse, at least—' Her voice shook. She turned away, climbing down.

'I have plenty of money now,' she said, when she had composed her face. 'At least I can buy a horse.'

Her twenty-first birthday, arriving two weeks after Will's death, had given her possession of her father's money at last. She had enough to buy whatever she desired. Her money could mend the fences and paint the stable doors, repair the drive, tidy the garden. She walked back to the house, white-faced, and stood looking at the open door, and the creeper swinging over the lintel, the windows blank, uncurtained. The blackbirds sang in the wild garden, and a pheasant croaked somewhere close, in the long grass. It was hot, and silent. Nothing moved but the bees in the willow-herb.

'I have plenty of money,' Christina repeated to herself. 'I can do anything I want.'

But the silence did not alter. Christina knew that Flambards was her own, to do whatever she liked with. It was there, in the sunshine, waiting for her to take possession.

'I can buy a horse,' she said to herself, 'but I can't buy *people*.'

No money on earth could buy the people she wanted.

Chapter 2

The sun went down over the high, flowering grass in the park in a thick pollen-heavy haze of golden light that hurt Christina's eyes. It was so incredibly still and untouched, the smells of the warm earth drawn out to meet the first chill of dusk, a yellow chestnut leaf falling, a rose petal hanging from a spider's thread, so infinitely uncomplicated . . . Christina felt she must be softened, eased by its peace. But she wasn't. It made her more bitter, this peace, that while she was standing looking at everything that was the essence of the sentimental picture of home, which all the newspapers made out that the 'boys over there' were fighting for, the fact that the boys over there were now dead and would never come home again made completely negative the sweetness of every flower and the balm of every sunset. Even worse, that the boys had not even paused to wonder if they were losing anything by dashing so eagerly to France; they had never noticed the sunsets when they were alive, save as portents of weather for a good flying day, or a good hunting day; they had gone happily, and been killed willingly . . . .

'No!' Christina caught herself up. Not willingly. Not in the hay-field, with the agony and skylarks mingled. Christina's face tightened. Oh, it was worse here! She should never—

'Miss Christina, dear, the tea's ready. I've made a nice bit of pie with a rabbit Fowler got, and gingerbread like you used to enjoy. We're a bit short on sugar, but all right for most things here, luckily. Come on in, dear; it's getting chilly. I've lit a fire in the dining-room, but I'm afraid it's smoking dreadfully. It's not been lit since the spring.' Mary was at her side.

Christina went to do her new duty as mistress of the household, to inspect the fire, and advise abandoning it, until the chimney should be swept. The dining-room, the one-time 'lair' of her Uncle Russell, the crippled father of Mark and Will, appalled her with its air of decay and smell of soot, the moths fluttering wearily against the window-panes, the dust thick on mahogany and leather.

'Oh, I don't want to eat in here! Let's eat in the kitchen, Mary.'

Their feet echoed across the tiled hall and down the empty passage. At least the kitchen, Mary's haunt, was warmed by the cheerful range; it was clean and scrubbed and homely. Mary would not eat with Christina, but waited on her until she had finished; then she ate her own meal at the other end of the table. Christina sat in the rail-backed chair by the range, watching the glow from the fire increase as dusk filled the big room. She felt very tired, and rather ill in an unfamiliar way, the rabbit pie lying uneasily. She did not feel capable, now, of deciding what she was going to do; she did not care. When Mary asked her, she shook her head, frowning.

'It's early days yet,' Mary said. 'It takes time. Fowler and me, even, we've sat here many a time and said we can't believe the two boys are gone. It just doesn't seem possible. This wicked war—' Christina had heard the platitudes a thousand times before: a million times, she thought—'taking our dear boys . . .' She shut her eyes.

'They *wanted* to go,' she said. 'They loved it. When Will came home on leave, he couldn't wait to get back.'

If Mary heard her, she made no sign, chatting on in the old-lady journalese that Christina had heard so often. Christina did not believe that anyone in that elderly generation could be expected to express a sensible opinion, and bore with her, not listening. How could Mary ever understand Will's passion for his work? No, he hadn't wanted to die for it, but he had willingly accepted every sort of privation the life offered, so that the ultimate sacrifice was, in a sense, a mere extension of normality. He had accepted as perfectly normal that one should enjoy going out on patrol at first light day after day all through the bitter months of December and January and February, when the casualties from frostbite were as many as those from gunfire and the agonies of the complaining circulatory system were to be suffered on every landing. 'I'd rather have it that way than moulder in a dug-out day and night up in the lines like the blokes we go spotting for,' he had declared. A hasty landing in flames a hundred yards on the right side of the lines had brought him home on an extended sick-leave twelve months after their marriage; five weeks, it was the longest period he had ever spent with Christina. They had rented a cottage in the Surrey hills, and walked and cooked and eaten picnics in the sunshine and talked and laughed. It was the happiest time they ever spent together, and yet, at the end of it, when Will had reported back to the Medical Board and was told he was fit for duty again, he had come back and told Christina not with regret but with the enthusiasm that she would always remember as his most endearing characteristic— in spite of the subject that invoked it.

'Back to your darling Morane!' she had teased. 'Oh, how lovely for you!'

'Yes, I'm throwing you over, Christina, for that heavenly little creature that always does exactly what I ask her.'

'She let you down, though—'

'Oh, well, she was badly treated. Make allowances. She doesn't make a habit of it.'

Christina had known when she had married him that she would never compete with Will's first love, but she had been secure in the knowledge that no woman ever would. And, because he had always been so happy to go back, their leave-takings had never been morbid or tearful. Her memories were all of laughing and teasing and cheerfully waving as some neat little machine skimmed away over the bumpy grass of a manufacturer's airfield. Even if she cried afterwards, she could only remember Will happy, which was what mattered. Even the last time, a fortnight before he was killed.

Mary was still talking.

Christina stared into the fire. The creaking house was full of ghosts, of the old man weeping over his brandy, the smell of the foxhound bitches, the great dinners of roast mutton after a day's hunting . . . she should never have come back.

'And there's no help to be had if you want it,' Mary grumbled on, like a squeaking cart-wheel. 'Even on the land, let alone in the house or the garden. The young men have gone, and even the girls are all in the munitions factories. Mr. Allington's land has gone all to rack and ruin since his boy went—Mr. Mark's land it is really, what old Mr. Russell let off to Allington after he couldn't work it no more . . . all weeds and thistles. . . .'

Christina remembered her vision of being a farmer, and shivered. Her trunks were in her room, unpacked, and when she went upstairs she made no move to take anything out of them, save her nightdress. She felt very cold and ill. Her room had the chill of decay in it, like the whole house, and the window was completely covered with ivy. It was like being in a tomb. Across the landing was Will's room, with the model flying-machines that he had made when he was little still hanging from the ceiling. 'I shall never go in there,' Christina thought. 'Never, never, never.' That was where she had first met him, lying in bed with a broken leg. She had been twelve, and he thirteen.

'If I stay here,' she thought, 'the ivy and the weeds will grow over me, too. Flambards is as dead now as Will and Mark. I will go away and if there is no word from Mark within the next month or two I will see the solicitors about selling it. I will see that Fowler has enough money to live on, and Mary; and Mary can have one of the cottages behind the stables. Then it will all be finished with. I shall never come back again.'

At least it would be a decision made, even if she still did not know what she was going to do. It was as if every road she turned to had a high, locked gate across it, erected as much by her own diffidence—and she realized this—as by circumstances. And the Flambards road, from which she had expected comfort, erected a barrier of impenetrable thorns. There was nothing here a mere girl could do; it needed an army of strong men. In her thoughts it had been a refuge; in fact it was a disaster.

'What a fool I was to come!'

The empty stables, the damp, empty rooms, revived memories that were no help at all.

She slept badly, and in the morning was very sick.

'I'll send Fowler for Dr. Porter,' Mary said, excited by having something important to do.

'It doesn't matter,' Christina said. 'I've had all this before. I had a doctor, and he said it was shock.' She wished she could die. If she did, there would be no one to notice that she had gone; she would disturb no one. It was raining, and the rain slithered over the ivy leaves, and did not touch the dust that filmed the window. Mary brought up a paraffin lamp, and Christina lay listening to the flame and the rain and the knocking of overgrown branches on the roof, smelling the damp and the mildew. She did not want to see Dr. Porter, another relic of the past, another old, old man. He had been old even when he had come before, for the boys' accidents.

When he came he shook her hand and made the same utterances of regret which Christina once more had to stiffen herself against. She started to tell him about her symptoms, to stop him, and repeated the opinions of the doctor who had seen her after Will's death. 'He said I was suffering from shock, but I don't see that I can be now. Not after six weeks.'

Dr. Porter examined her, and she lay and looked up at the damp on the ceiling, and thought of Will with an impossible longing. 'I hope he will tell me that I'm going to die,' she thought, and she had a picture of Will laughing, waiting for her. 'How can it be shock?' she thought. She had been prepared for it for four years, ever since she had loved Will and he had flown aeroplanes.

'No, it's not shock,' Dr. Porter said. 'You are going to have a child.'

He smiled at her. Her face stared back at him, as white as the pillow beneath it.

'It's not death that is upsetting you, my dear. Quite the opposite.' He turned and rang the bell-pull beside the bed. 'I'll tell Mary to bring you a nice strong cup of tea. It's a great surprise, I can see. Had it not occurred to you?'

Christina, with what felt like her last ounce of strength, shook her head. The tears poured down her cheeks, like the rain over the ivy leaves. No wonder Will had been laughing! She could not say a word.

Mary came in, her eyes curious.

'There's nothing wrong, I hope?'

'No, oh no,' Dr. Porter said. 'Nothing that time won't cure.'

Time, to Christina, lost all meaning. She lay curled up in her bed, glad of the ivy blanking out the cold light of day. She wanted nothing and no one, only the blessed peace of the musty room. Ironically, she was now suffering from shock. Mary thought she had a stomach upset and lit a fire in her room and brought her meals up, but otherwise left her to rest. (She was very happy having someone to nurse.)

So much for her indecision, Christina thought. Now it was all decided for her. But after the idea had taken root, she could do nothing but give herself up to a fresh, agonizing, useless, involuntary grief for Will, as bad as the first, when the telegram came. It was no good trying to fight it; it flooded her. She lay staring into the shadows, remembering all the inconsequential moods of their brief marriage, the tears running sideways into her hair and her ears. She despised herself, and cried on. And all the time she could not understand why the news made her feel so sad; she thought it ought to make her feel happy. She tried to tell herself that it was Will all over again, that she would never be lonely again, as she was now. But her inner sense only told her that any characteristics of Will's the child might show would merely serve to remind her of Will himself; that a child's company was an unmitigating bore for years. She had never had anything to do with children, nor particularly wanted to, and had never wished for a child when Will was alive, feeling that it would merely come between them. Will had never raised the subject and Christina guessed that, if it had been mentioned, he would have shown no interest. (If it had been a new prototype from the Royal Aircraft Establishment, he would have discussed it for hours.)

Then, after the first orgy of self-pity, other considerations groped into her mind.

She stopped crying, and lay watching the soft light from the paraffin lamp. If she had a child, most of the alternative courses of action were closed to her. She could hardly go back to her job as a hotel receptionist, or become a nurse like Dorothy, the daughter of her old employer. She could not work in a munitions factory, nor did she think she would be particularly welcome at the home of her Aunt Grace, a hard-working dressmaker in Battersea. For a child, she would need a home.

'Flambards,' she thought, 'will belong to this child.'

It was all. The child would have no father, no grandparents, no brothers, sisters, aunts, uncles, or cousins. It would have two old great-aunts—and Flambards. Christina's pity transferred itself to the child. She lay very still, appalled for this child. She saw it forlorn in the great wastes of crumbling Flambards, with a mourning mother and the ancient servants for sole company. The picture was so stark that Christina sat up in bed, pushing back her damp hair.

'Flambards *must* come to life again. I cannot leave it to fall down. And I cannot sell it, for no one would have it.' Now that Mark was dead, it was hers, for what it was worth. She had no choice any longer. She pushed her feet out of bed, scrambling for her slippers.

'There is so much to do! I cannot waste time here. What a fool I am! Oh, what a fool!'

Chapter 3

'The two boys from the village are outside now, ma'am, if you want to see them.'

Fowler stood at the kitchen door, very formal with disapproval.

'It's all there is to be had, ma'am, and I don't see as how you'll ever make farmers out of either of 'em.'

'Show them in.' Christina was equally cold. Both Mary and Fowler were appalled at the plans she had hatched in her sickbed, and had taken no pains to conceal the fact. Fowler, his old face twitching with horror, had poured scorn on her plans. 'Make Flambards pay! Why, it didn't pay even when Mr.

Russell was in his prime, and it was a twelve-horse farm! A lady like you can't be a farmer!' He had been so moved that all his years of 'begging your pardon, ma'am' and 'if I might say so, ma'am' had been thrown to the winds. He had stamped up and down the kitchen like a demented goblin. Now, having made his feelings clear, he was very correct again.

Mary said, from beside the sink, 'You can't interview staff in the kitchen, ma'am. It's not right. Have Fowler show them through the front door into the dining-room.'

She sniffed tartly. She was on Fowler's side all the way.

'Very well.' Christina was not disposed to argue about so minor a detail. As she crossed the hall she thought, 'How impressed they'll be by such grandeur!' A pile of fallen plaster lay on the cracked tiles at the foot of the stairs, and when she opened the dining-room door two mice scuttered away into a hole in the floorboards. 'Oh, how elegant!' Christina said out loud. There was a glistening of fungus on the wall over the fire-place, and the ornate ceiling was hanging in stained bulges. It was dark, like her bedroom, with the inroads of the ivy, and the heavy furniture lowered in the gloom. Christina could not bring herself to sit down. She stood with her back to the fire-place, like a man, and Mary showed the two village boys in.

Christina saw immediately, with a surge of anger towards Fowler, that one was an idiot. He looked about thirteen, and had a large vacant face and a happy smile. He was built like a young bull, with long arms and huge hands which lolled at his sides. The other character was by comparison very sharp-looking, with reddish-brown hair brushed back and insolent, quick eyes that looked Christina smartly up and down. She felt instantly antagonistic towards him.

'What have you done before?' she asked sharply.

He told her his history, which made out that he could do everything. His name was Stanley Minton, and the idiot he referred to as Harry. Harry said nothing, but smiled.

'Why aren't you in the Army?' Christina asked Stanley.

'I'm not daft, mum.'

Christina frowned, instinctively repelled by the slick tongue. But the boy was obviously strong and quick. If he was honest, he could be a good worker. Christina very much doubted whether he was honest.

'I'll try you both for a week,' she said. 'Call tomorrow at six, and Fowler will tell you what to do. I'll pay you twelve shillings, and I'll raise it if you're any good.'

'Very well, mum.'

Stanley's eyes slid all round the decrepit room as he took his leave, shoving the cheerful Harry along in front of him. Christina went back to the kitchen, stubbornly angry. Fowler was drinking tea with Mary. They stood up when she came in.

'Is it that bad?' Christina said to Fowler. 'Are there only idiots to be had?'

Fowler had the grace to look slightly shamefaced. 'Yes, ma'am,' he said. 'It is that bad. You can try yourself, and you'll do no better. There's only dregs. Young Minton was in munitions, but he got the sack. He can work if he wants to, but he needs watching.'

'It will be your job to watch him, then,' Christina said. 'When they come tomorrow I want you to put them on to stripping the ivy away from all these windows. Even the idiot should be able to manage that.'

'Yes, ma'am.'

Christina felt no compunction about being hard on Fowler and Mary. They infuriated her with their stubborn antagonism. She realized now that they had wanted her back, so that the responsibility for the place would be taken from them, but they did not want anything else to change. They wanted, perhaps, a smart horse, and a kitchen-maid, and new gravel on the drive and paint on the doors, but no more. They did not want to fight, only moulder on their way. They did not know the reason for Christina's new determination, and Christina had no intention of telling them.

'And, Fowler, I want you to find me a builder who will come and do some work here.'

'It's very difficult to find a—'

'It may be very difficult, but I want you to find one.'

'Yes, ma'am.'

'And that horse, Pepper—has he carried a side-saddle before? Can I take him out?'

'Yes, ma'am.'

'Get him ready for me, then.'

She went upstairs to change into her riding-clothes. At least

17

she might as well find out the extent of her acres, and just how many weeds they grew. 'And I cannot live in the kitchen,' she thought. 'If I'm going to act like the lord of the manor, I must have my own room downstairs.' But she could not face the vast desolation of the dining-room. It could never be anything to her but old Russell's lair, and she did not want his spirit breathing over her every movement. (Although, strangely, she knew that old Russell would approve of what she was doing, had he the power to see her from his seat in heaven—no, Christina corrected her thoughts—in hell. Old Russell would surely not have gone to heaven.)

'I should have started the boys on the ivy today,' she thought as she went downstairs. A cheerful noise would have improved the place enormously. She kicked the fallen plaster out of her way and stopped, one hand on the banister rail. A faint sunlight struggled in over the front door, showing gracious proportions, and the skeletons—beneath flaking paint and dog-scrabbled panels—of fine doorways. She remembered how once she had pictured it like a hall in a lady's magazine, with bowls of flowers, and calling-cards on a silver plate, and a maid in a black dress. 'Why not?' she thought grimly. She opened the other doors, peering in. One room was almost filled with a billiards table, its green baize in tatters. A lot of old harness was slung over some chairs and a chaise-longue with burst stuffing filled the window bay. The other room had once been used as a study; Christina had done lessons there herself with Mark and Will. She opened the door, recalling a smell of ink and an atmosphere of ill will, but the room had been cleared of its tables and chairs, and all that remained was a sofa and a faded golden-coloured carpet. The room was small, and looked out over the park, through windows that stretched round in a pleasant bay. It had a plain marble mantelpiece, and tiles round the fire with gold roses painted on them. It faced south, and smelt of trapped sun.

'Why, this is all right.' Christina was pleasantly amazed. 'This could be a nice room!' She looked round with her first lift of pleasure, almost excitement. She saw it as a gold room, looking out on to the chestnuts, the brown paint changed to cream, the evening sun slanting in, gold on the gold carpet.

'Yes, this will be my room!' She saw herself eating tea by the

18

fire, interviewing farm-labourers with bulging muscles and honest faces, recording her bushels of wheat in a ledger . . . 'I *will*,' she thought.

She went out through the kitchen, and gave orders to Mary to clean the room out, enjoying the old woman's look of rage.

'Oh, I am hard,' she thought. 'I shall make it come right. I shall make it all work, and be a proper farmer, and learn to ride astride.' For a few minutes it would work, this enthusiasm, if she concentrated on it. But if she let her mind stray . . . The quicksands lay all round, waiting to take her.

Fowler, looking more cheerful, had Pepper ready saddled in the yard. The horse was a dark bay with an honest head. Dull. In old Russell's days the driving-horses and the hunters never mixed jobs. Now Pepper, like Fowler, did everything.

'Can you plough, Fowler?' Christina asked.

Old Fowler's face gaped.

'I'm not a—'

'Can you plough?'

'Yes, ma'am.'

Christina smiled. 'We must buy some horses—cart-horses, I mean. Will you find out if there are any sales on, and let me know?' Her eyes fixed him.

'Yes, ma'am.'

'I'm going up to look at the farm, to see how bad it is.' The farm buildings that belonged to Flambards were on the other side of the covert, almost a mile away.

'It's in a terrible state, ma'am. Mr. Allington patched the stables a few years back, but you couldn't put a horse there and expect it to thrive.'

'We might have to use these stables, in that case.'

'For the cart-horses!' Fowler's face went bright red. Christina watched him struggle with his emotions, little threads of outrage pulsing on his temples. He led Pepper up to the mounting-block, and she climbed up and settled herself in the saddle.

'You say you don't know who bought Woodpigeon, only that it was a doctor?'

Fowler, tightening the girths, replied, 'A doctor out Woodham way. I don't know his name.'

'See if you can find out, will you?'

'Very well, ma'am.'

Christina rode out away from the house, through the big fields where she had learned to ride with Dick, and into the covert. Pepper was a quiet, stolid ride—'Very suitable for my condition,' Christina thought, with an odd stir of emotion at the thought. But it was her fields she wanted to think about. '*My* fields,' she thought, 'and this is *my* covert. All these trees are mine, and the pheasants and the foxes and the rooks and the moss and the toadstools.' She was a landowner, rich and powerful. 'That is what I must think about,' she thought, 'not all the other things.'

When she came out of the ride at the other side she saw the fields spreading away, thin barley marbled with weeds, and uncut hay splayed by the rain, divided by hedges twenty feet high and ditches brimming with nettles. It was lush and profligate. Neglected. Beyond the farthest corner of weeds a ring of old elms marked the site of the village church, and a few roofs crouched beyond the hedges, showing where the road lay. The home farm lay in the midst of its shameful crops, a cluster of picturesque barns and tiled roofs. A lane bordered with elms led away from it towards the road, and another track came up a slight hill to where Christina sat at the edge of the covert. It looked pretty from a distance. Christina would have liked to turn back and keep the image in her mind, but she pressed Pepper on and went down the track at a canter.

At close quarters the farm could only be described as dilapidated, if not derelict. The farm-house, a four-square brick building with a sagging roof, stood in a small garden of nettles and elderberry with railings round it. Beside it the duckpond was choked with reeds, and tenanted only by mallard and moorhens; and high grass had flowered over the cart-tracks that wound into the stockyard. Pepper made a swathe through it like a horse on a prairie. The wagons stood in the barns with oats and grass growing out of the floorboards where the seed had sprouted, and the rows of scythes hanging from the rafters were rusty and spattered with pigeon droppings. There were large pieces of machinery which—beyond a couple of ploughs—Christina was unable to put a name to, all very dilapidated, and in another shed rows of harness, too old ever to use again, layered over with dust. The empty stables, with holes in the roof, and the empty threshing-barn with its great timbers arching up into the gloom, silent and bare like a medieval church, laid a cold hand over Christina as she rode the carriage-horse from door to door. The silence was oppressive. The flowery heads of the big thistles floated away on the summer breeze,

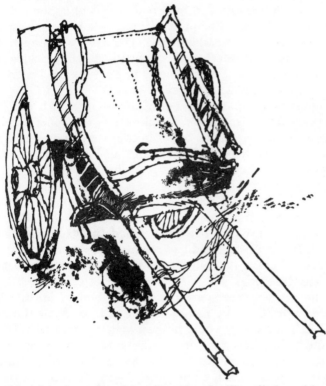

brushing her face, dissolving into the sky like all the wishes she had once dreamed up for her life. She stroked Pepper's neck, pursing up her lips. She could see what she was up against now, more than any words of Fowler's could have told her.

'Oh, come on, Pepper!' She would cry again, in her feeble way, if she stayed in this sad place. 'It will be all right,' she thought, 'when there are men there and horses and the roofs are patched up . . . and *people*. It's always *people*,' she said to Pepper, with a desperate swallowing of a sob. 'It wants people!' Pepper fled up the dry track at a gallop, feeling her urgency, his head stretched out, his stiff old legs stirring the dust, the barley barbs tossing in his wake. 'It will be all right,' Christina said to him, her hands holding his hard old mouth. 'It will be all right, Pepper, given time.' Nothing, as Dr. Porter had said, that time wouldn't cure.

Riding, at a more sedate pace, along the peaty track through the covert, she was startled by a bounding and crashing in the undergrowth behind. She pulled Pepper to a halt, and waited, rather nervously, to see what it was. There was a whimper, and then a noise that left her in no doubt at all, pricking her memories like a spur. Pepper's ears pricked up and he snorted with excitement, pawing the earth.

The foxhound that came out of the undergrowth was in a state of complete exhaustion. It lolloped up to Pepper and laid its muzzle on Christina's ankle, looking up at her with an expression—half hope, half fear, and all bewilderment—that went straight to her heart.

'Oh, you poor thing!'

She slid off Pepper and held her hand out, but the animal cringed back as if it expected a blow. It was as thin as a rail, with bramble tears all over it, yet had the look of a young animal. It was a bitch, and had the markings typical of the old Flambards hounds that old Russell had devoted a good deal of his life to breeding.

'Who are you, then, my poor dear?' Once Christina had known each hound by name, but she did not know this one. The bitch would not come near now that Christina was dismounted, but cowered under the bushes, backing away. Christina sensed that it would follow her, and walked on, leading Pepper, and the bitch came slowly, very nervous. Christina wanted it to come desperately; it was young and in trouble, like herself, and it was a bit of the old Flambards that had got steamrollered by events. It followed, and Christina walked on through the covert and across the fields, back to the stable-yard. The bitch came into the stable-yard some thirty feet behind her, and stood watching.

Fowler came to take Pepper.

'Do you know that bitch?' Christina asked him. 'She's in a dreadful state.'

Fowler looked, and considered.

'Looks like young Marigold to me, as went to Suffolk when Mr. Lucas went away.'

'Marigold?'

'Daughter of Matchless—you'll remember Matchless? And Matchless was by Marmalade, your uncle's darling.'

'Yes, I remember Matchless.' Matchless had been one of Mark's favourites, as Marmalade had been his father's; Mark had laid bets with young Allington on Matchless's owning first to a line, Christina remembered. Marigold's pedigree was peerless.

'Looks like she's come down from Suffolk on her own, to me,' Fowler said. 'She's in a bad old way.'

'She's come to the right place, then,' Christina said. 'We'll keep her; she belongs here.' She felt excited; Marigold was a part of the re-peopling of Flambards, materializing out of the covert as if by act of God. 'I'll go up to the house and get her some meat. She looks starving.'

The bitch ate and drank, and fell into an exhausted sleep in a corner of one of the deserted loose-boxes. Christina walked back to the house, glad about the hound, pleased that by tomorrow the boys would be at work on the ivy, that there would be some signs of life about the place. Although Flambards had been neglected when she had lived in it before, there had at least been coming and going, the boys in the stables, and Violet in the kitchen; doors slamming and hoofs crunching on the gravel. 'It will happen,' she thought. 'It will improve . . .' And in the train of thought Violet's face lingered. Christina stopped beneath the deep shade of the chestnut-trees, and a jumble of memories turned themselves over in her head. Here, on this very spot,

23

Dick, the kindest and most intelligent of all the stable-boys, had kissed her when she had cried for her mare, Sweetbriar. Dick had been Violet's brother, Fowler's favourite, the one who had been dismissed for doing Christina a favour against old Russell's orders, the one whom Mark had hated. And Violet—Christina stood in the drive, seeing nothing, biting her thumbnail . . . *Violet!* The sudden, unbidden memory of what had happened to Violet now had all the relevance in the world. Christina's eyes widened with sudden excitement. She turned and ran up to the house, and went into the kitchen without bothering to change first.

'Mary, I want to ask you something. What happened to Violet?'

Mary gawped at her. 'Violet?'

'The kitchen-maid. She was dismissed because she was going to have a baby. You remember?'

'Of course I remember,' Mary said, her old lips closing in an angry line.

'What happened to her?'

'I'm sure I don't know,' Mary said, as adamant as Christina herself.

'Don't you know whether she had the child? What happened to it?'

'No, I don't. I wasn't interested, ma'am, I'm sure.' Mary's voice was tight with disapproval.

'Oh, how can you *not* be interested?' Christina was angry with Mary's anger. 'It was Mark's child, wasn't it? That's what all the trouble was about, and why Dick came back and had that fight with Mark, wasn't it? Why else, then, if that wasn't the reason?'

Mary's old-fashioned disgust seemed to Christina infinitely petty beside the stark fact that Mark, who was dead, had left a child. She could not understand the mentality of the old woman, to be so prudish about this past history, when any birth—however irregular—was surely a more welcome subject of conversation than death, which she would gladly discuss for hours.

'I would like to find out what happened to the child. Who would know?'

'Nobody as I know of. Violet went to London—that's all any-one knows.'

'And Dick joined the Army. Violet would be Dick's next of kin, so her address should be in the Army records.' Christina, talking to herself, went upstairs to get changed. She was taut with excitement. The door of her sitting-room was open and a smell of scrubbing-soap permeated the hall, and the disturbed moths were blundering about the cornices, but Christina did not notice. She was thinking of the phantom people, the anonymous child, six years old, the ghost of sobbing Violet . . .

It could come right, if she was clever enough. There were threads to follow: even Marigold was a part of it—and Woodpigeon, pulling the doctor's trap. 'I will buy Woodpigeon back, and find Violet, and *buy* Mark's son off her, and there will be two children here, and the fields all ploughed and the lawns all smooth . . .' It was like a dream, what she saw in her head, the children's faces laughing, a groom holding their ponies at the door, bowls of flowers in the hall—like one of old Mary's novels, like an illustration in a magazine.

'Why not?' Christina said fiercely to her reflection in the mirror. The reflection should have stared back, all fire and resolution, but it looked frightened. Why not indeed? The reflection trembled at what was being asked of it. It was a thin, white-faced reflection, all eyes and cheek-bones and tumbled untidy hair. And when it stood still, listening, its dream faded, and the house was empty and cold as a tomb.

Christina, having found out from Fowler Dick's regiment, wrote to Colchester Barracks, and received a terse reply to the effect that they could not enter into a correspondence concerning next of kin of Trooper Richard Wright.

She showed the letter to Fowler. They were in the dog-cart at the time, on their way to a farm sale, to see if there were any horses. Christina was handling the reins, with Fowler beside her watching her performance, fairly cheerful and apparently resigned to the day's work.

'Hmm,' was Fowler's comment, frowning over the message. Christina remembered that he had cried when Dick had been dismissed.

'I never had another boy as good as Dick,' he said, handing the letter back. 'Never will, either. He just knew horses. It was in him.' He spat into the road.

'Where else can I find out where Violet is, then? There must be someone who knows.' Christina was confident that Fowler knew why she wanted to find Violet, although she hadn't told him.

Fowler, watching her hands on the reins, said, 'Mrs. Masters might know. She used to visit old Mrs. Wright when they moved her to the workhouse, after Dick and Violet had gone away.'

'Mrs. Masters?'

'They have a farm over Mickleditch. Young Amy used to go out hunting—you'll remember her?'

'Yes, I remember Amy.' Amy had been a tough young blonde with an eye for Mark. 'I'll go and see her tomorrow.'

'That's a farm, now—Mickleditch,' Fowler said. 'They say he's making a fortune, with the wheat prices what they are. Both his boys are still at home, working, and even with conscription come in he's got them deferred. There's no flies on Masters.'

Christina hated the young men who stayed at home, alive, when Will was dead.

'Eighty shillings a quarter!' Fowler sighed.

'We'll get that next year,' Christina said angrily.

'If it comes up, we will.'

The statement was indisputable, and Christina said nothing.

'Make him stride out a bit more, Miss Christina. He's lazy, this one, if he has the chance.'

The farm where the sale was being held was swarming with hopeful buyers. Dog-carts jammed the lane, with bicycles threading their way through, pedestrians tramping over the verges.

'You can see how things have changed, eh? You never saw this before the war.' Fowler, in his element, had forgotten his original doubts, and even his deferential manners. Christina was pleased, almost amused, wondering if he would unbend enough as time went on to handle a plough, and be horseman to a team of Punches. They left Pepper with a nosebag, and went round the yards on foot, searching out the horses.

'Horses and harness to go with 'em, Miss Christina. That's what you want. Our machinery can be fixed; it's not too far gone, and you can get your cattle off Masters or Discoll, nearer at hand.' Fowler led the way, catalogue in hand.

Christina, at last, was not unhappy. She knew what she wanted, and she liked the bustle and the smell, and the feel of belonging to this crowd, because she was after a bargain the same as all the rest of them. Fowler knew the horses that were

for sale, and shoved his way into the barn where they were tied up, awaiting the auctioneer. Christina followed, happy to leave the choice to him. Her mind was roving, for all the business in hand, and kept going to Violet and the child. Violet had become very clear in her memory, and Christina's imagination had provided a sweet-faced child, whom Violet would weep over.

Violet had been an intelligent girl, intelligent enough to realize that her child would have a better chance in life if it went to live at Flambards. Christina's heart was set on it, and the Violet of her imagination was not allowed to oppose this desire. Christina, looking at horses, was taut with a purpose that had nothing to do with horses. It was something quite unexpected that brought her mind back to the day's task.

'Oh, Fowler, look! Who's this?'

There were twelve farm-horses in a long row and at the end, in the corner, a riding-horse. It stood turned towards the on-lookers as far as its tight halter would allow, its nostrils dilated with apprehension, as if at bay. It was obviously a well-bred animal although not very big; 'a lady's hunter', Christina would have thought an appropriate description, save for the fact that the white-rimmed eye and sweating shoulder suggested an unladylike temperament. It was a rich bay in colour, with dark mottles on its coat, as if it were standing under the shade of a tree.

'Who does it remind you of, Fowler?' Christina asked eagerly.

'Treasure, ma'am, to be sure. A little Treasure.'

'That's what I thought. Show me the catalogue. What does it say?'

Fowler showed her the entry, muttering a reminder: 'We're here for the farm-horses, miss, if you remember.'

The horse was entered briefly as 'Argus Pheasant, bay gelding by Black Argus, 14.3 hands, 5 years'.

'I want a riding-horse, Fowler.'

Fowler scratched his nose, saying nothing.

'He's a lovely horse.' Christina was confident that Fowler could not deny this. The horse was both compact and refined, with hard, wide quarters, thick through the chest, but with a fine, arched neck and a beautiful head. There was a narrow stripe down the face, ending in a pink snip on the muzzle, but all the points were black, and the feet hard and shapely. The animal stared at Christina, and she saw the red nervousness in his nostrils and the shadows in his eyes. 'He's been ill-treated,' she thought. 'Like me.'

'I shall buy him,' she said.

Fowler looked gloomy, and clicked his tongue against his teeth. 'There must be something wrong, or the Army'ld have had him by now.'

'He's too small.'

'They take them all sizes and conditions these days, except dead.'

Christina was impatient with Fowler's caution, and excited about the eager little bay. She allowed Fowler to pick his plough animals, acknowledging his judgement as he lifted enormous feet and ran his skinny fingers down the knotty tendons.

'They've all seen too much work,' he said, but Christina was confident, her mind on the bay.

'Buy which you want,' she told him.

'I reckon they'll fetch high prices. You should put a top

mark on them, ma'am. We don't want to regret anything.'

'We must have them. You bid for what you want, and I'll pay for them. And Argus Pheasant, remember.'

'If you say so, ma'am.'

When the bidding started she was all impatience for the thirteenth horse. Fowler, by judicious nods of the head, bought Dolly, Punch, Jack, Boxer, Dusty, and Ginger, obviously stricken by the prices he was paying, and Christina felt her responsibilities gathering, her commitments starting, with a feeling more of foreboding than excitement. But for the thirteenth horse her eyes gleamed.

'He's not a lady's horse, ma'am,' Fowler said, as the gelding was led into the dusty yard. The buyers who had pressed round for the heavy horses were silent in a way Christina could not define. The horse, nervous at the crowd, stood with his head up, ears twitching, his eyes quick with fear. Christina was moved by his beauty, the perfect balance of strength and refinement, and the arrogance of his stride.

'Looks aren't everything, Miss Christina,' Fowler said. 'He's a bad 'un—I'd lay a bet on it.'

'We'll bid for him,' Christina said, very sharp.

The auctioneer asked for a bid. A voice from the back cried out, 'Two and a tanner!' and there was a yelp of laughter. The auctioneer glared. After a long pause, someone offered two pounds, and the price rose spasmodically to twelve. Fowler offered thirteen. 'It's all thirteens with this horse,' he muttered to Christina. 'I don't like it.' Christina, anxious now, eyed her competitor. He was a wiry man, with a face like a ferret, eyes like nails. She knew that all the silent bystanders knew more than she knew about the horse; he was worth, by the present-day standards, ten times the last bid. He fell to Christina for fifteen guineas. Fowler shook his head.

'That's a bad day's work, ma'am.'

Christina, knowing from the low price that Fowler's fears were certainly well founded, pushed her way angrily through the crowd. She paid her cheque to the auctioneer's clerk and went to where a groom stood holding Argus Pheasant. Several people watched her, smiling.

'What's wrong with him, then?' she asked. She felt shaken, sick with disappointment.

'He's a bit funny in the head. Times you can't do anything with him, ma'am.' The groom was grinning.

'Why? Has he been knocked about?'

'Not the last year or two, but before that I reckon. He sees ghosts, the master says.'

Christina stroked her horse's neck, and he turned and pushed at her hand, eager and gentle at the same time. Christina adored him, but the disappointment was like a lead weight in her stomach. She felt bitterly angry at the workings of fate, yet—strangely—would not have changed the afternoon.

'I'll manage,' she said.

'The master thought that,' the groom said. He was a young Fowler, Christina decided, stolid with country fatalism . . . mud clods in the brain . . . She had forgotten, after all the years with Will, how the country people kept their feet on the ground. With Will nothing had been impossible, not even flying in the sky. His feet, literally, had left the ground. The thought came like a shaft of sunlight—winter sunlight perhaps—to hearten her. A little courage was all that was needed. She took the horse's halter. She was aware of several men watching her, and knew that they were summing her up because she was presuming to become a farmer. Her fierceness touched the new horse, and he walked obediently beside her, to where Fowler was waiting for her. Fowler, she knew, would already have found out what she had just learned.

'We'll take him home with us, behind the dog-cart. The boys can fetch the other horses in the morning.'

'Very well, ma'am. When I've bid for the harness . . .'

'Yes. I'll walk him round until you're ready.'

Christina was not interested in the harness. She led Argus Pheasant out of the yards and into the field where the dog-carts and wagons were lined up by the hedge. There were only two motor-cars; one was Mr. Masters's. 'You wait, Mr. Masters. One day I shall drive to sales in my own motor-car,' Christina said to the smart Ford. It would not be for preference, only to show status, and her success with wheat. Will had taught her to drive a motor-car. A picture of Will, leaning out of Sandy's Model T with his arm stretched out to pull her up, his dark eyes laughing, cap on back to front, came into her mind very suddenly, very vividly. For a brief instant Will was as near and as real as he once had been in fact. Christina gripped the horse's halter, and shut her eyes, but the dream was past almost before it had come. Her mind reached to recall the vision, frantic, but it was irrevocable, dissolved like thistledown.

The horse started to graze. Christina stood desolate, feeling as if her heart had been wrenched out. 'Why now?' she said aloud, and leaned her face on the warm, shining back, her arm hanging over the withers. Just at that moment she had had no reason to recall Will, her new life taking shape with more urgency than at any time during the last few months. It took a vast effort of will-power not to be shattered, to straighten up from the horse's back and remember where she had been before the motor-car had so fatally distracted her. She had been happy, almost, in those few minutes before the groom had told her the truth about Argus Pheasant.

'It shows I can be happy now, if I want to be,' she told herself firmly. She stared at her horse, and saw his pink muzzle eagerly searching the autumn grass, his nervous eye moving back to watch her. 'It will be all right, Argus Pheasant,' she told him. 'You must make things come right, whatever those bumpkins say. You've got to cheer me up. You and my wheat.'

What a dangerous vessel to put her hopes in, she could not

help her mind adding—a horse who saw ghosts! 'We both see them. We've got something in common, you and I, Pheasant,' she said. She followed his slow search over the pasture, the halter in her hand, remembering Violet again, and her own child, and all the things that made up her future. Even Marigold. Fowler was a long time. Christina pulled Pheasant up from his grazing and led him back towards her dog-cart. Coming towards her over the grass was a vaguely familiar figure, a girl of about her own age, with a tall, hard-faced, middle-aged man. A farmer, Christina thought, rich by the look of him . . . the girl used to hunt . . . Amy Masters. Christina turned her horse and went to intercept them, acting on an immediate impulse.

Masters recognized her.

'Mrs. Russell?' He smiled and looked quite pleasant, while Christina remembered the sons he still had at home, making money, instead of getting shot at in France.

'I wanted to see you, Mr. Masters—about—' She hesitated.

Masters, apparently not in a hurry, said, 'I hear you're going to farm Flambards. Is that right?'

'Yes. I'm going to try.'

'If there's anything I can help you with, you must let me know. I'm not too far away. It's nice to see you back again, although I'm very sorry, of course, about—' He went red, breathing heavily with embarrassment.

'It's men to do the work that seems to be the biggest difficulty,' Christina said hastily, changing the subject to the first thing that came into her head.

'Yes, you're right. I'm afraid that's one thing we're all in trouble with. I'm not down to taking Hun prisoners yet, though! There's no one round here will touch 'em so far.'

Christina never knew such a thing was possible. How ignorant she was! Her bad buy, in the shape of Argus Pheasant, which both Masters and his daughter were eyeing with interest, embarrassed her in front of these professionals.

'We came to get cart-horses,' she explained. 'I wanted a riding-horse, too, but it seems he hasn't a very good reputation. It's rather late to have found out.'

'Funny things, horses. You might make something of him— he's young, isn't he? You won't get a better looker.'

Christina decided that Masters might not be so bad after all.

'That's what made me want him. He reminds me of Treasure, Mark's horse; do you remember?'

'Yes, you're right! There is a resemblance. Same blood somewhere, I dare say. What's the news of Mark, by the way? Have you heard anything from him?'

Christina saw Amy's eyes turn abruptly away from the horse and meet her own.

'No. No.' The brief moment of optimism was stamped out, again, quenched by reality. 'I wanted to ask you—' Oh, how difficult it was! 'Fowler told me that Mrs. Masters might know where Violet went to—where she is now—'

'Violet?'

'She was the kitchen-maid at Flambards, before the war. A long time ago.'

Masters looked baffled. 'I'm afraid I don't know anything—'

'I remember who you mean,' Amy said. Christina saw by Amy's eyes that Amy remembered everything. She said stiffly, to put Amy off, 'I want to get in touch with her about a legacy. And no one knows where she is now.'

'My mother had her address. It's in London somewhere—unless she's moved.'

'Could I ride over for it tomorrow?'

'Yes, of course.'

'Come for lunch,' Masters said. 'Would twelve suit you?'

'Thank you very much.'

Christina felt that she had accomplished more that day than in all the others she had spent at Flambards. If only Will's ghost had not touched her, that moment in the field, she would have been happier than for a long time. She sat in the dog-cart, watching the new horse trotting uneasily behind, listening to the two sets of hoofs on the hard road: Pepper's steady and confident, and Pheasant's uneasy, uneven. She felt for Pheasant, she talked to him soothingly as they bowled along, and Fowler, shaking Pepper's reins, shook his head and whistled between his teeth.

Chapter 4

Christina rode over to Mickleditch on Pepper, although she would have dearly liked to try Pheasant. Fowler promised to have him ready for her to ride when she returned—'In the park, ma'am, with myself to hand to pick up the pieces.' (Fowler seemed to have become more outspoken since the even tenor of his old age had been disturbed; Christina liked this, and realized—with less approval—how much she was coming to depend on his advice.)

She would have liked to be on Pheasant, purely for reasons of vanity, when she rode into the Mickleditch yard and one of Masters's sons, Edward, came to take her reins. She had been spoilt in the past by the quality of the horses old Russell had provided for her to ride; she found Pepper's lethargic paces and hard mouth very dispiriting. A little part of her mind flickered with anticipation at the thought of getting home and trying Pheasant, even while she was greeting Edward.

Masters had three sons, Edward, Herbert, and Percy. They were strapping physical specimens, quietly spoken, but with sharp, intelligent eyes. They were intelligent enough, Christina thought, to stay at home; with all the ardour of her age and experience she hated them for this. While Edward put Pepper away for her, she stood in the yard watching the harvest teams moving down the lane beyond, taking the wheat to the rick-yards where it was being unloaded and built into perfect ricks. Christina had guessed that Masters's ricks would not be the sort that sagged and had to be propped up with timber; they were meticulous and there were rows and rows of them . . . the wagons swayed past, pulled by teams of gleaming, fit horses, two men to each wagon, besides the rick-builders.

Edward rejoined her. 'We're taking advantage of the weather.

It's been a wicked wet harvest this year. I can't remember such a bad one, and no sign of a settled period ahead either. Ploughing will be all behind.' He smiled at her. 'Not a very good year for you to start, the land being so wet.'

Christina thought of her dusty horses and the dilapidated ploughs in her barn and her three ploughmen: the ancient, the miscreant, and the idiot. 'No,' she said.

Edward escorted her to the farm-house, a rambling ivy-covered building not unlike a small Flambards. But only in the architecture was there any affinity. Mrs. Masters, a small, hard-bitten, very efficient woman, was supervising the serving up of the lunch, which was laid on a big scrubbed table in the middle of the kitchen. A cook was dishing up a leg of mutton and a kitchen-maid was putting out vegetables, whilst another woman had come to fetch beer for the harvesters. The Masters boys were washing in the scullery; Amy was fetching an extra chair. Christina had not seen so much activity for weeks. The serving of the food was being effected with the same speed and efficiency as the harvesting of the crops.

'My dear!' Mrs. Masters came forward to receive her. Christina could see that she was shrewd and energetic, as essential a part of the Masters machinery as the farmers themselves. It was as if all the ingredients of the successful farm were being displayed for her own benefit: the number and nature of the people employed, their attitude to their work, and the equipment all in perfect order, the intricate, timeless getting of the harvest proceeding all to plan, even while the master took time off to eat his meal.

'We always eat lunch in the kitchen. You'll excuse us! But just as well you came for lunch, because at this time of year the men are nearly all asleep by dinner-time.'

'It was very kind of Mr. Masters to invite me.' Through an open door across the hall Christina saw the dining-room and the solid mahogany and the port decanters, dusted and bright with use.

The men came to the table and they all stood while the father said grace. Not shutting her eyes, Christina watched them and sent up a man-to-man prayer that was nothing to do with food: 'Oh God, I wouldn't have swopped any of them for Will. Thank you for Will.'

'Amen!' said Mr. Masters.

He started to carve, very quickly and easily, and said to Christina, 'So you are going to be a farmer.'

She listened to his advice all through lunch, not daring to speak in case she showed her terrible ignorance. She seized on a few points to pass on to Fowler, such as the hiring of a steam-plough for the initial opening up of the land, but for the most part let it ride over her head. All the time she was very conscious of the strong Masters boys, proud of their cunning in evading conscription, pleased with the prices they were getting for their wheat. If it hadn't been for Will and Mark, Christina felt that they would have boasted to her about their skill and good fortune, but, as it was, she could see that they were faintly embarrassed when the question of labour was raised. She was glad when they all excused themselves from the table, and left her with Mrs. Masters and Amy.

'Now, it was that girl's address you were wanting?' Mrs. Masters said. 'Go to my bureau, Amy, and bring me my diary for—let me think—the year Mrs. Wright died . . . eleven, I think it was, Amy. I'm sure I jotted Violet's address down at the time. We'll soon see, anyway.'

'Five years ago,' Christina thought. A lot had happened in five years. Violet might prove elusive.

'She went to London when she left you, I know that. She was in trouble, I believe. Dick going, and then Violet, was the death of Mrs. Wright. She had nothing else to live for.'

'No.' Even now, after all that had happened, Christina could feel the awfulness again, of Dick being dismissed through some-thing that had been entirely her fault. She remembered Dick's golden hair when he had taken off his cap to go and see Mr. Russell; she remembered Mark laughing, and Will defending Dick, and getting beaten for his pains. . . .

'It was very sad,' Mrs. Masters said.

'Yes.' Christina felt the guilt, like a sickness, go through her again. She and Mark between them had been the ruin of that small family and even now she was only wanting to see Violet for her own ends, not in any way to help Violet. 'But I *do* want to see Violet,' Christina thought stubbornly. It was no good wavering, being soft. The child had become too real to let go now. It was lodged in Christina's imagination as surely as her own was in her body.

Amy brought the diary and handed it to her mother. Christina knew that the mother and daughter were both thinking of the reason why Violet went away, but politely not saying anything. It was Mark's ghost this time that was very close, careless, amused. In the arrogant Russell manner, he had never given a thought to Violet after she had gone away. She had been paid off and sent packing, and that was the end of it.

'Thirty-six Waterhouse Street, Rotherhithe,' Mrs. Masters read out. 'I'll write it down for you.'

Christina took the piece of paper.

'I'll go tomorrow,' she said. 'It's very kind of you.'

Her mission completed, she took her leave as soon as she decently could. Amy went to get one of the men to fetch Pepper, and Christina rode away from the farm through the fields where the harvest was being taken. She was excited and tensed up, her mind all bound up with the child. It had been so long since she had had anything to look forward to that she felt quite strange, as if she had turned into somebody else. Her mind kept running away with her, thinking of herself with this ready-made child. And in this vision the child was sweet-faced and smiling, with—in spite of the fact that it was a Russell—the same blonde hair as Dick and Violet; it held her hand as they wandered through the park, and the park was mowed and smooth and the fences neat, and the sun shone. The child was a girl, just as the child that she was going to bear was, she felt convinced, a boy. It was with a sense of shock that she rode into the stable-yard and saw Fowler with the new horse saddled and bridled, ready to be led out of his box.

'I saw you coming up the drive, ma'am, and I just put a bridle on 'im. I had 'im all ready for you.'

He held Pepper while she slid down.

'Oh—thank you.'

She had almost forgotten. She waited while he put Pepper away, trying to gather herself together. She felt very tired again, and unreal, almost dazed. The bitch, Marigold, was lying in the autumn sun beside the trough, watching her. 'Oh, what does it matter?' Christina thought inconsequentially. 'Nothing really makes any difference. Everything will happen how it is meant to happen. I cannot do anything to change it.' Whether Pheasant was any good or not, or whether she found Violet, or whether the child existed; whether she was to succeed or fail with her farm . . . She took off her hat and repinned her hair, which was falling down on her neck. What did it matter?

Fowler led Pheasant out. The little horse watched her nervously as she came up to him. Fowler got him to move over against the mounting-block, and Christina noticed how neatly he crossed his legs, turning on his forehand, arching his neck to the bit. His coat shone like silk. Fowler had obviously been spending some time on him.

'The boys have gone to fetch the cart-horses, ma'am. They should be back soon. Eh up, young fellow. You're a lady's horse now.'

Christina got into the saddle. She had only ridden proved horses before, and was aware of a slight doubt as she picked up the reins. What she was doing was not wise, all things considered, but—if Fowler thought the same—it was not for the same reason that was in Christina's mind.

But Pheasant, nervous and kind together, walked without seeing any ghosts, round and round the small paddock behind the stables. Fowler shut the gate and stood watching, and Christina rode, feeling she was on the edge of a precipice. Not only in Pheasant's uncertainty, but in what was going to happen. She watched the horse's mane blowing in the breeze and felt the horse's doubts and her own working together, just as the warmth of their two bodies mingled where her leg touched his side. They neither of them knew what was going to happen. Christina put the horse into a trot, sitting firmly down in the saddle. He had a long, smooth stride, but there was this hesitation, a sense of anxiety about what lay ahead of him, and behind him. There was no relaxation in riding him.

'I don't know about seeing ghosts, but you're certainly looking for them.' She pulled him up and stroked his neck. His behaviour was so akin to her own mood that she could only think of it as appropriate. There was nothing to censure. He was perfectly obedient.

'He's all right,' she said to Fowler.

'All right now,' Fowler agreed.

He could be all right for ever, if she were lucky, just as Violet could be found tomorrow, if she were lucky . . . Christina had this strange feeling that everything was out of her hands; it would happen, or it would not happen. She did not want to talk about farming, or about the boys, who were still away fetching the horses. She went back to the house, to look out some suitable clothes for going to Rotherhithe.

It rained again the next day, and Christina gave a passing thought to Masters's harvest as she rode in a hansom cab across Tower Bridge. The yellow river with its scum of filth seemed very far from the gold wheat of Mickleditch, yet the same wheat could find its way up here quite easily; several of the barges below were full of grain. Masts and yards reached up to dull autumn clouds; tug smoke and factory smoke mingled. Christina watched the rain spiking the water and shivered. It was like Battersea, where she had gone with Will after they had run away; the smell of the river, whiffs of sulphur and gas and brewing, stirred memories best forgotten.

She had dressed carefully, to appear authoritative and prosperous, but fairly inconspicuous. She felt like a governess as a result, in severe dark grey (save that she was showing, perhaps, a good deal more ankle than a governess might, even allowing for wartime freedom in dress). She was nervous, very depressed, and excited all at once. She sat in the cab screwing her gloves in her fingers, wondering if she was making a terrible mistake in what she was attempting to do. 'But Violet will have gone,' she reassured herself. 'I am getting worked up all for nothing.' The patient cab-horse wove its way past several drays and a steam wagon, crossed some jolting tram-lines, and continued its weary trot down a cobbled road lined with shops. Nothing Christina saw cheered her up at all: the shabbily dressed women clutching their straw shopping-bags—any of them could have been Violet, for they were all grey-faced and anonymous in the rain. The cab pulled up for a tram, then turned off down a street of small, mean houses. A left and a right, and Christina saw the name Waterhouse Street. The doors opened straight on to the worn pavement flags; broken gutters deluged rain-water down the pitted blackened brickwork, runnelling the dirty window-glass where grey curtains moved with curiosity to the sound of a hansom. A sodden newspaper flapped across the cab-horse's foreleg, cartwheeling out of an overfull dustbin. 'Hard fighting round Thiepval.' The lettering mashed into the cobbles, and the cabman shouted down to Christina, 'Number thirty-six, ma'am!'

'Wait for me a moment,' Christina said to him.

She could not stop shivering. Number thirty-six was no different from any of the other numbers. Its windows were as dirty, the paintwork peeling. Christina raised the knocker and let it crash. It made a hollow noise, as if there were no carpets inside. A man and woman walked past her on the pavement, staring hard.

After what seemed to Christina a very long wait, she heard feet shuffling behind the door, and the door opened. A woman of about twenty-five, wiping her hands on her apron, looked at Christina sourly. She took in Christina's dress, and the hansom cab, with an expression of surprise, which gradually changed to one of servitude, and then apprehension.

'What d'you want?'

Christina knew at once that it was Violet, and the shock of it almost took away her powers of speech.

'Vi—Violet—' She swallowed, to make her voice come right. 'Do you remember me? Christina?'

'Oh Gawd!' Violet's already pale face went white. 'Yes! Oh, miss—ma'am! Oh, whatever—'

'Can I speak to you?'

'Oh, yes, ma'am, come in, do, I'm sure—'

Christina paid off the cab, her fingers trembling with excitement. She was astonished at finding Violet so quickly, as shocked as Violet looked. The thought of what she was going to ask Violet made her feel sick.

Violet was saying, 'You'll have to excuse this place, Miss Christina—ma'am. It's just a pigsty. If you'd like to sit here a moment, I'll just see to the children—'

Stepping inside, Christina could understand Violet's harassed looks, for the house was not designed for entertaining. The fire that burned in the grate was entirely invisible behind the banks of steaming washing hanging in front of it and from the ceiling above it, and the rest of the room was filled by a large dining-table covered with a tatty velour cloth and the chairs that stood round it. A coloured engraving of Queen Alexandra on one wall stared at Christina as she edged her way in.

'I'll just move some of the washing, so's you can see the fire. This weather's such a ——.' Violet used words that surprised Christina, although she did not show it. She only thought that, perhaps, if she lived in such conditions she might use the same words. A glimpse through the open door into the kitchen showed a chaos of brimming sink and buckets, something boiling over on the stove, a baby strapped in a chair eating bread and jam, and two other children playing at the sink, screaming with laughter. They were girls, with long blonde curls. Violet, having revealed the fire, turned her attention to them, silencing them with brusque slaps.

'Give us some peace now!' she told them sharply. 'I'll give you a penny and you can go and fetch me a basin of pease pudding at the shop. Get your coats!'

Behind smears of jam, the little girls had thin, pretty faces, blue eyes all curiosity. Christina watched them closely, hearing her own heart beating with nervousness. The eldest looked smaller than she had imagined, but, even in her grubby pinafore and broken boots, she had a charm that encouraged Christina. Her tangle of uncombed hair was the colour of Masters's harvest.

41

Violet quickly submerged this attractive-
ness beneath a torn coat several times too big
for the child and an ugly bonnet. The other
one similarly garbed, they were both shooed out into the rain
and the door slammed behind them. Violet put a kettle on
to boil, scooped up the baby, still with bread and jam, and took
it up the uncarpeted stairs which opened out of the living-room.
Presumably it was put into a cot, from where it cried for the
rest of the time Christina remained in the house. Christina
thought of her own baby, and realized that she knew very little
about children at all. Compared with Violet, who handled them
with such careless disregard, she was a complete beginner. This
thought did not increase her confidence.

'There, we might get a bit o' peace now,' Violet said. 'They drive you mad this weather, under your feet all day.'

Violet was thin to the point of gauntness, the prettiness that Christina remembered quite vanished. Her fair hair was dulled and her cheeks fallen in. Her face in repose had a look of permanent worry, which had made lines across her forehead. Christina remembered her watching Mark, and the glow that had lit her, touching her with beauty. It seemed impossible now.

'I'll make us a cup of tea, ma'am. I'm sure you could do with it, if you've come far.' The remark was questioning.

'I've come from Flambards,' Christina said.

'Why, are you back there, then, ma'am? I heard as you'd gone away, with Mr. William—'

'Yes. We got married, but he was killed, so I've gone back. Old Mr. Russell is dead, so there's no one else there now. Only Mary and Fowler.'

'I'm sorry, ma'am.' Violet's voice was quiet. Christina knew what she was thinking.

'Mark is dead, too,' she told her, to get it over. 'He was reported missing after the fighting round Gaza. That's all I know. We've not heard another word.'

Violet did not say anything at once, and there was a long silence which Christina did nothing to break. Having known the facts herself for some time made them no less bleak now, and in the silence she felt very close to Violet.

Eventually Violet said, in a flat voice, 'Well, he was the sort, I suppose. Not to sit back, I mean, and let everyone else do it. I've often wondered . . .' Her voice trailed away. There was another, shorter, silence, then she said, almost vehemently, 'Well, it was a long time ago. I've been married twice since then. He's not the only one I've wept over, believe me. I'll make the tea.'

She made it, very strong, in a brown teapot and brought cups and saucers and sugar and a jug of milk and set them on the table. The fire was now burning cheerfully; the rain rattled on the window-panes, and Christina's nerves were soothed. It was homely, amongst the washing, stirring the thick tea. She could say it now.

'Really, I came to see whether—to see the child, Mark's child.' She felt her cheeks flushing as she spoke.

Violet gave her a surprised, suspicious look. 'What do you want with him, then?'

'Him?' Christina was surprised, too.

'It was a boy.'

'I thought—I assumed it was the girl—'

'No. The girls were born when I was married to my first husband. He was killed at Mons and I married his brother and we had the baby. The story of my life in a nutshell.' Violet sighed, as if the recounting gave her little to congratulate herself upon.

'Where's the boy now, then? Does he live with you?'

'Yes, he lives with us. Now he's where he always is, I suppose. Up at the brewery.'

Christina, who had worked out that the child was not yet six, was puzzled. 'The brewery?'

'He hangs round the stables there all day long. The carters take him out with them. He's a proper little ——.' Violet used the same words as she had used earlier for the weather.

'I wanted to take him back to Flambards.' Christina decided not to hesitate. She felt that Violet, having obviously had several knocks in her life, was a person one could approach squarely. She looked too tough to be shocked by the suggestion. Also instinctively, after Violet's description, she did not want to flinch from the plan herself. This prompted the rather brutal announcement of her reason for coming.

'Well!' Violet was startled. 'You mean—'

'There's nobody left now. I thought, if he could grow up there, he could take Mark's place. He could have everything he wanted. I would pay for it all. In fact, if you agree to let me adopt him, I would pay you a sum of money to make it worth while.'

'How much?' Violet asked sharply.

'Five hundred pounds.'

Violet stared into her cup of tea, and stirred it absently. Then she tapped the teaspoon in the saucer and stared out of the window.

'We could use five hundred pounds,' she said.

She got up and went to fill up the teapot in the kitchen. She was very slow, and came back without saying anything, her eyes far away. She poured Christina another cup, and herself,

and stirred sugar into the fresh cup. Christina sat listening to
the rain, and the puttering fire, and felt that time had stopped
moving. She felt numb, almost as if it didn't matter very much,
whatever Violet decided. Although it had mattered, earlier.
Then the feeling came again, as it had the day before, that it
was all out of her hands, that nothing really mattered any more.
She let her breath out with a sigh, and knew that everything
would take its course, one way or the other. She would adjust to
whatever Violet decided.

'My husband wouldn't be sorry to see the back of him,'
Violet said, 'but—' And she stopped. Whatever she had been
going to say she bit off abruptly. An expression crossed her face
that Christina remembered strongly from the days when she
had been the kitchen-maid; it was what she had thought of as
Violet's sly look. 'Violet is hiding something,' she thought
instinctively. And again, 'But what does it matter?'

'It's up to you,' she said to Violet.

'He's been nothing but trouble,' Violet said. 'Jack'ld give
him away for five hundred pounds any day of the week. But—'
She caught herself up again. 'So would I,' she added. 'I've got
more on my hands than I can manage, without him.'

There was another long, heavy silence. Christina said,
because she felt she ought to, 'You should discuss it with your
husband before you decide.'

'Oh, no. *He* would have the money, no argument. So would
I, come to that. It's—' She paused. Another silence. Then
Violet pushed her chair back abruptly and said, 'We'll go and
fetch him, shall we? Or would you rather wait here?'

'I'd rather come.'

They went out into the rain, leaving the baby crying upstairs. The low clouds, mingled with smoke, made it seem like
dusk, and the smell of the river came with the rain, and the
smell of breweries and drains. Christina held her smart umbrella
over Violet. All her smart clothes were left from the Hendon
days, before she was married, when she had gone to watch Will
give flying exhibitions. It seemed like fifty years ago. 'Whatever
am I doing?' she wondered, avoiding broken flags, feeling the
water splashing the backs of her legs. Nothing was real any
more.

They came down into a busy street, waiting on a corner for

the horse traffic to go past. Behind them, the Red Lion was doing a busy trade. Over the cobbles and down a street flanked with warehouses; then Christina smelt the familiar warm smell of stables, and Violet passed through high gates into a brewery yard. An empty dray followed them through, pulled by a pair of bay Shires, and they had to draw back against the wall; opposite, another dray was loading, the horses champing their bits impatiently. They were magnificent animals. Even now, with quite a different excitement inside her, Christina watched them admiringly, appreciating the work that went into such a turn-out. A warmth touched her, that the child was drawn to this place, and she looked eagerly for a sight of him.

'Is Tizzy here, Bert?' Violet called to the men loading.

The men, staring at Christina, shouted back, 'He's out with Charlie.'

Violet swore. 'Will he be long?'

'No. Short haul. Another five minutes, perhaps.'

'D'you mind?' Violet asked Christina. 'He's not back till dark as a rule. The men give him bread and cheese, he's not bothered with his dinner. And it suits me.'

'No—'

Christina drew back as another dray swung in at the gates.

'This is Charlie,' Violet said.

Up beside the driver sat a small figure with a sack over his head. Already, before the horses had stopped, he was scrambling down like a monkey, running to their heads.

'Tizzy's ma wants him, Charlie,' the men shouted, and Charlie swung round to Violet with a grin.

'What'll I do without my mate, then?'

Violet swore again, not amused. 'Tizzy!' she shouted angrily across the yard. 'Come here, before I come and clump you. We haven't got all day!'

The figure turned, dropping the traces that he had already unhooked, and came with obvious reluctance, glowering. In his expression Christina saw Mark, facing his father after some misdemeanour, clenching his hands as if he already felt the cane. The features were so alike, and with them the same strong similarity to Will, that Christina was taken off her guard. She pressed back against the wall, feeling that she wanted its solidity to hold her, and stared. Tizzy stared back at her with exactly Mark's candour, tinged with insolence. His eyes were the Russell almost-black, his hair black and curling with the rain. (A faint, faint memory of a sweetly smiling blonde girl-child stirred in Christina's mind and sank, for ever, without trace.)

'Who's she?' Tizzy said to Violet.

'Mind your lip,' Violet said sharply. 'You're coming home with us.'

Tizzy stuck his underlip out and glared. 'I don't—'

Violet's hand shot out and struck him smartly across the cheek, leaving red finger-marks. Tizzy's eyes filled with tears—physical, involuntary tears from the blow rather than emotional tears, for his truculence remained undoused. He went on glaring murderously at them both. Violet turned round and marched out through the gate with a sharp 'Come along.' Christina, after a moment's doubtful hesitation towards Tizzy, followed her, and Tizzy trailed behind, muttering. Christina's emotions were in a turmoil. She held up her umbrella and saw the traffic as if through a fog. A tram's jangle stopped her. She waited with Violet on the kerb, trying to gather her wits.

'We're lucky he wasn't out all day,' Violet said tartly, hauling the child across the road by the arm. 'All the menfolk in my family are the same—only in for meals. Bellies and bed—it's all they think a home's for.'

She kept up a tirade all the way home, holding Tizzy's wrist in a grip that whitened the flesh over the bones. When they got to the door she flung Tizzy inside ahead of her and stood back for Christina to go in. Seeing the velour table-cloth and the stale teacups, and the steaming washing, Christina felt a frantic desire to clutch Tizzy as tightly as Violet herself had done and run.

'I won't stay,' she said, trying to keep her voice normal, not to show that all her wits had proved ungatherable. 'If you agree, I'll write you a cheque, and take him home with me now. A solicitor will draw it all up so that it's legal.'

'Yes, I agree.'

Christina wrote the cheque, after Violet had gone to borrow ink, and left it on the table. Upstairs the baby was still crying and in the kitchen Tizzy was quarrelling with the two girls who had returned from their errand. Violet went in and hit him again, and stood him against the sink and scrubbed his face and hands.

'Go and fetch your best boots,' she commanded him, having rubbed him violently dry.

'Why? Where are we going?'

'You're going with this lady.'

'I don't want—'

'Do as you're told!' Violet's hand shot out again, but this time Tizzy stepped back in time, and ran for his boots.

Christina stood waiting, cold inside.

In a few minutes Tizzy stood before her, an incongruous

little object in his best clothes, his hair parted and flattened, his face trying to show defiance, but not succeeding very well. He looked very small and vulnerable. 'Whatever am I doing?' Christina thought desperately. The two girls stood staring, their fingers in their mouths.

'Where's Tizzy going?' the younger one asked.

'Tizzy's going with this nice lady,' Violet said. 'I've made a parcel of his clothes, ma'am. If—' Her rough voice trailed off. Tizzy was looking at her hopefully, two large tears swelling on his eyelashes. Christina thrust out her hand, and took Tizzy's.

'Come on,' she said. 'I've got eight horses. I'll show them to you.'

Tizzy came. Violet pushed the small parcel towards Christina and opened the door. Christina did not dare look at her.

Violet said, in a choked voice, 'His name's Thomas—Thomas Mark.'

'I will get in touch with you,' Christina said, 'as soon as—'

Instinct told her not to linger. Violet's haunted face seemed to follow her all the way down the street. Tizzy half ran at her side, his hand still in hers, and she could not tell whether the wet on his cheek was rain or tears. Nor on her own either. 'What have I done? What have I done?' she kept thinking. She walked very quickly, panic-stricken. Somehow there was a tram, and on Tower Bridge a passing hansom where Tizzy wanted to sit with the driver. At Liverpool Street Station, Christina showed him the trains, but he preferred the cart-horses. Christina was comforted.

'What's your horses called?' he asked her.

Christina tried to remember, and made up what she had forgotten. 'And Pepper and Pheasant—they're riding-horses.'

'Can I ride Pheasan'?'

'You can ride Pepper.'

'I wan' to ride Pheasan'.'

'All right. But he's very—' She hesitated. What was he very? She had yet to find out.

'Is he a ——, like Tiger?' He used a terrible word, worse than Violet's.

'Yes,' Christina agreed. 'He's a ——.'

Tizzy sat on the train seat, his thin legs swinging. His nose was running, and he wiped it on his sleeve. When the train started to move he scrambled up and put his head out of the window.

'Mind your—' Christina started, but she was too late. The cap with the hard new peak had already fallen off and lay beside the track like a busker's appeal. Tizzy withdrew and cringed, a look of animal terror on his face.

'It doesn't matter,' Christina said.

'I didn't—' His voice was a wail. 'It fell—it—'

'It doesn't matter.'

He looked utterly bewildered. Christina watched him, shattered again by the familiarity of his features. The wind caught his flattened hair and it started to spring up. 'Whatever have I done?' Christina thought again.

Chapter 5

'Oh, my God!' said Mary when she saw Tizzy, and went as white as a sheet. Christina had to fetch her some of old Russell's brandy, which still stood in a decanter in the sideboard. Fowler, whose reaction had been exactly the same, stood in the kitchen, wiping his feet, grinning and agitated, turning his cap round and round in his hands.

'He's a right chip off the old block and no mistake, 'strewth. Eh, Mary?'

Mary started to cry. Christina, who was tired and had a splitting headache, wanted to shout at them.

'Have you got something for tea?' she asked Mary.

'It's in the oven.' Mary scrambled to her feet, dabbing her eyes. 'Oh, ma'am, how could you do such a thing? And him nothing but a little b——'

'Don't you dare say that!' Christina said, turning furiously on the old woman. 'Get the tea before I throw something at you! Don't you ever say anything like that again.' She felt close to tears herself, exhausted by the day's events. How ridiculous, now, if they all sat around crying. . . . She straightened up firmly. 'Take your coat off, Tizzy.'

'Tizzy?' Mary repeated, not beaten. She slammed plates down on the table. 'What sort of a name is that?'

'His name is Thomas,' Christina said, dropping down on one knee to undo his coat buttons.

'It's Tizzy,' he said.

'Does everybody call you Tizzy?'

'Yes. I wan' to see Pheasan'.' He looked at Fowler and added, 'She says Pheasan's a—'

'*Tizzy!*' Christina drowned the word, hastily snatching his coat. 'Come and sit at the table now.'

Fowler was chuckling. 'Well, I'll be—'

'Get out,' Christina said to him. 'Get out!'

'You sit down, ma'am,' Mary said, reversing the roles abruptly. 'You're tired out, I can see. I'll see to the young brat. Come and sit here, what's-your-name, and mind your manners. You're in a lady's house now.'

Christina, not caring any more, sat at the table and watched Tizzy adjusting to this new person. A cautious appraisal of the situation seemed to come naturally to him; she guessed that he had learned, through an instinct of self-preservation, to judge the adult humour. He watched Mary with his bold Russell eyes, and Mary kept darting him unbelieving glances, clicking her tongue under her breath, and muttering every now and then. Tizzy ate loudly and enthusiastically, his head well down to the plate, elbows out. 'Like Marigold,' Christina thought. When he had finished he said, 'I want to see Pheasan'.'

'It's dark now,' Christina said involuntarily.

'You *said*.' Tizzy glowered at her.

'Yes, I did.'

They went out into the autumn evening, Tizzy holding

Christina's hand. A great gold harvest moon, like something theatrical, hung over the covert, and an owl sent out its eerie, wintry calls, as if stage-managed for Tizzy's benefit. His hand tightened in Christina's.

'What's that?'

'An owl.'

'What's nowl?'

'Just a bird. You don't get them in cities.'

'Where's the lamps, then?'

'You don't have lamps in the country. The moon does.'

'It smells.'

Christina smelt the great autumn primeval smell of everything that was wet and earthy and dank, that smelt of leaves and dripping webs and trodden fungus and all the rotted, wet, decayed things of years, decades, and centuries back, and said, 'Yes.' A sense of time and inevitability, of becoming fungus in one's turn, as old Russell had done and his great-great-grandfather, as Will had and she would, and Tizzy, too, in his turn, went through her with piercing sad nostalgia. The owl and the moon were no help at all, nor Tizzy's trusting hand.

'Look, here are the stables.' She was glad to pass through the gates and take Tizzy across the yard and into the silent building. The moon shone through the windows and showed the row of empty boxes, the railed tops gleaming. But Pheasant and Pepper gave low, welcoming knuckers, turning their heads round from the hay-racks, and Tizzy went forward eagerly. Christina saw the look of surprise on his face.

'They're cab-horses. Little horses.'

Christina, remembering the brewery Shires, laughed at his disappointment.

'Not cab-horses! Not Pheasant, anyway. He's a thoroughbred —almost a thoroughbred, at least. Look at his lovely head.'

Tizzy looked. 'You said eight. Are the others big? Where are they?'

'They'll be over at the farm.'

'I want to see them.'

The day had been so strange Christina saw no reason why it should not continue that way. She bridled Pepper and led him out into the moonlight, beside the mounting-block. She got on him, astride, so that the legs of her drawers showed beneath the

bunched-up skirts of her governess dress, and pulled Tizzy up
in front of her, astride over Pepper's withers. He was warm and
thin against her, sitting confidently, as he had obviously sat
many times on the Shires.

'You can ride,' Christina said.

'Yes.'

They rode out of the yard, heading across the field for the
track through the covert. As they passed through the gate a pied
shape detached itself from the shadows and ambled beside them.

'That's Marigold, my foxhound bitch.'

Tizzy wriggled with excitement.

'Can I have her? D'you want her?'

'You can have her, if you want.'

'Does she chase foxes?'

'That's what she is bred for.' What did the child know about chasing foxes, Christina wondered? The moon shone above them like a reading-lamp, picking out every blade of yellow grass, every shrivelling oak leaf. It was quivering still, bright and strange. Pepper went obediently, and passed into the mysterious gloom of the covert, his hoofs making no sound on the peaty path. Christina felt Tizzy tense with nervous curiosity. Marigold ran backwards and forwards, casting, halting, and leaping through the undergrowth. Her cheerful hunting, rattling through the wood, was a relief to Christina, breaking the spell of the silent covert.

'There. You can see the farm, at the bottom of the track.'

They came out of the wood and the fields of abandoned barley spread like a silver sea before them. Tizzy, to whom the scene was as utterly incomprehensible as the sea itself would have been, said, 'What is it?'

'What's what?'

'It. All.'

'It's fields of corn. Barley. Barley is what beer is made from. What your horses carry on their drays.'

Pepper went down the track and Marigold ran on ahead, plunging in and out of the hedge. Webs of cloud passed over the moon, and cleared, and they came down to the farm buildings and saw the holes in the thatch and bulges in the walls as clearly as if it were daylight.

'It's old, your farm,' Tizzy said.

'Yes. It needs mending.'

But it was not so dead, now, as it had been before, with the six horses in the stable. The smell was of living animals, not just rot and mustiness, and as they went in through the door the steady sound of munching was comforting. Christina noticed that the moonlight shone in through the holes in the roof, out-lining the motley half-dozen. Even before Tizzy said it, she saw that the horses were very humble compared with his Shires.

'You'll have to be my horseman,' she said to him, 'and make these horses all smart and shining.'

She had no horseman, she remembered. Neither Stanley nor Harry knew how to look after horses, and old Fowler was past keeping eight horses without help, even should he condescend to do the farm-horses at all. The tatty harness lay in tangled heaps on the floor, where the boys had dropped it. The leather was cracked and the buckles rusty. For a moment it was as if the merciless moon was picking out, spotlighting, her formidable problems, mocking the dusty, work-worn horses in the stable, and swilling the acres outside, right to the farthest corner of the farm, to show her how much work there was to do. Masters's mention of the word 'prisoners' came into her head. She stood there, her mind turned from Tizzy to this basic problem.

'I shouldn't have come,' she thought. 'I didn't have to remember all this tonight.'

There was enough without it. But Tizzy was happy. They rode home, Marigold running ahead, and Christina let Tizzy lead Pepper into his box, and take off the bridle. Pheasant whinnied over the partition, his white blaze gleaming in the dark.

'Will you feed the horses for me tomorrow?' Christina asked Tizzy.

'Yes. An' can Marigol' come back with us? Will that old woman mind?'

'No.'

It was almost too good to be true, that Tizzy was content to stay. Christina took him up to bed, with some bread and jam and Marigold, silencing Mary's protestations with a glance. Mark's bed had been made up and a hot bottle put in to air it—the only sign of comfort in the comfortless room, Christina noticed with a pang. Mark had never been one for frills; his room, exactly as it had always been, was decorated solely by mounted foxes' masks, snarling from the walls, and the solitary silver cup that Treasure had won in the point-to-point in 1913.

'What are them things?'

Tizzy, looking ridiculously small and lonely as he sat up in the huge, sagging bed, eyed the masks doubtfully.

'Just stuffed foxes.' Christina, aware of their unsuitability in making a small boy feel at home, tried to dismiss them as if they were of no importance. 'Look, Marigold will stay in your room with you. She can sleep by the bed, and you can talk to her. I'll leave this candle burning.'

'What's that jug?'

'That's a silver cup that was won by a horse called Treasure in a race.'

'Did you ride him?'

'No. Your—' She very nearly said, 'Your father rode him', but stopped herself in time.

'Can I ride him?'

'No. He's gone to the war.'

'Can I ride Pheasan'?'

'Perhaps.'

'Tomorrow?'

'We'll see.'

She backed to the door, shaken more than she could have imagined by the sight of Mark's infant in Mark's bed. Her plan had worked with diabolical success. She felt utterly exhausted, all her emotions used up.

'Hi, missus!' The voice called her back when she was half-way down the stairs. She went back.

'Can I ride Pheasan' in a race?'

'Yes.' She was more weary than he was. She went to bed and slept without dreaming, until an ice-cold hand laid itself on her cheek and a hoarse voice said, 'I don' like them foxes.'

Standing in the white moonlight, Tizzy wept, the tears rolling out of his dark eyes. Marigold stood anxiously by him pushing her muzzle at Christina's face.

'Oh, Tizzy!' Christina lifted up her blankets, making a black, warm cave for him. He scrambled in and snuggled up to her, and Marigold put her front legs on the bed, wriggling with excitement.

'Get down!' Christina said to the bitch. 'Don't cry, Tizzy. You can stay with me.'

'I wan' my Uncle Dick,' he said.

'Your—' Christina started up, only to be instantly over-whelmed by the arrival of Marigold. One clumsy paw almost went in her mouth. She beat at the bitch, shoving her plunging friendliness aside.

'Get off, you brute! Down! What did you say, Tizzy? Who do you want?'

'I wan' my Uncle Dick.'

'But your Uncle Dick is—' Is what? Christina pushed Marigold off the bed. 'Tizzy, where's your Uncle Dick? I thought he was—'

'M'Uncle Dick's at home.'

Christina lay back, shaken. She was as much shaken by her own lurching emotion at Tizzy's mention of Dick as by the news that Dick was at home.

'I thought he was in the Army. I thought he was abroad.'

'He come back. Can Marigol' come in the bed?'

'No, she can't. What does your Uncle Dick do now, then? Is he working?'

'He goes in the Red Lion.'

It was Dick, then, who wouldn't have sold Tizzy for five hundred pounds, the reason for Violet's hesitation. Of all the ironies in life, Christina considered the one revealed by Tizzy: that Dick and Tizzy were friends—and Tizzy was the son of Dick's great hate in life, Mark. It was because of Dick, not because he was his father's son, that Tizzy was drawn to the brewery horses, that he knew about foxhunting.

'Does your Uncle Dick tell you about horses?'

'Yes.'

'He used to be a groom here. When he was a boy.'

'No, not here.'

'Yes, he did.'

'He was a groom at Flambar's.'

'This is Flambards.'

'Oh, no, it isn't,' Tizzy said. 'Can Marigol' come up? She wants to come up.'

Marigold came up, wriggling against them, all hard bone and sinew. Christina, pushed on to the far edge of the bed, heard Tizzy's breath lengthen into sleep, and thought of Dick. She thought of Dick all night, and slept when it was almost dawn.

The possibility that Dick, of all people, might come back to Flambards to help run the farm was in Christina's head constantly. Now that the horses had come, the farm was a reality, no longer just an idea. Immediately, there were the horses to be fed and groomed, the stable roof to be mended, the harness got serviceable and the farm paddock securely fenced so that the animals could be turned out until the machinery was ready for them to use. All the machinery needed attention. The blacksmith and the wheelwright came up to look it over, and Christina drove over to the office of the steam traction company, whose address Masters·had given her, to see about a gang coming to plough up the Flambards weeds. The same day Fowler went to see Masters about buying cattle. 'We shall never do it all, with only Stanley and Harry,' she thought. They had cut back the ivy and hacked the garden away from the terrace, and now it was their turn to become farm-hands proper. There were the hedges to cut and burn and the cattle-yards made secure. Harry did whatever was asked of him, slowly, happily, and to the best of his ability, and Stanley appeared to work very hard, but in fact got very little done. Christina had the harness moved into the kitchen and worked on it herself with neat's-foot oil, evening after evening.

'I'm going to ask the Agriculture about getting prisoners,' she said to Fowler, having made up her mind. They were in the kitchen, having lunch.

'Prisoners! Huns!' Mary turned round from the stove, glaring. 'Here in Flambards? After the dirty swine killed your own husband?'

'It's highly unlikely that I shall be offered the dirty swine that killed Will,' Christina said, in a voice that silenced Mary.

'It'll be a sad day as sees a Hun set foot here,' Fowler said stubbornly. 'There's no one round here stooped to it yet.'

There was a silence. Christina would not argue, but her face was stony. She thought, 'If Dick would come and work here . . .' She still had not discovered why he was no longer in the Army, for Tizzy did not appear to know. She presumed he had been invalided out. Day after day she had almost made up her mind to go and seek him out, and day after day, for a reason she could put no name to, she put it off. She was frightened of what, in the past, she had done to Dick, and the thought of facing him again made her sick with panic. Worse than when she had gone to seek out Violet. 'But *that* was all right,' she reasoned with herself. 'Why not this?' And she knew she would never rest until she had seen him again.

'I will see if Dick will come, and if not—' She shrugged.

Soon, too, she would have to tell them why she was putting on weight. This would be a shock of a different kind; Christina reckoned that Mary would require the brandy bottle again.

Hammering noises came from the hall, where an ancient builder was slowly doing the repairs, helped by Tizzy and

Marigold. Plaster and wood-shavings were trailed through the whole house; the dust lay in thick layers. And in what Christina hopefully thought of as her sitting-room the builder's grandson, a boy of twelve, stripped paintwork with an enthusiasm that would score the panelling for the rest of its days. The carpet was rolled up out of the way and the wormeaten floorboards gaped, half knocked out, the new timber stacked ready. Christina, worried and tired, listened to the noise that—a few weeks back—she had so desired, and longed for peace. With the child becoming a reality inside her, she now wanted to withdraw, to dream, to reflect upon this strange act of nature, so commonplace and yet so utterly uncommon in its effect upon her feelings, but because of the child she was committed to this turmoil. 'Never satisfied,' she said to herself. But at least she had overcome the habit of grief. The letters, the unofficial and the official, and the telegram which started, 'We regret to inform you that your husband, Captain William Edward Russell, D.S.O., was killed in action . . .' had been locked away.

Fowler, tuned to complaints, said, 'And you must decide what you want to do with that funny-tempered gelding, ma'am. He needs more exercise than you're giving him, or we'll have trouble.'

'Oh, Pheasant . . .' Christina had found she could ride Pheasant, and he saw no ghosts, and went kindly. That and Tizzy were the two great slices of luck which had come her way, the two gambles that had come off. Fortune, after all, was not entirely against her.

'We can't ask anyone else to ride him, the way he is, and I'm too old to care for the likes of him. Old bones don't mend easy.' For Pheasant, who went for Christina, had seen enough ghosts when Fowler had ridden him to put the old man off for life. He had shied at a pigeon and bolted and Fowler had not been able to pull him up for over a mile; then, coming back, he had taken exception to a gateway and refused to pass through it. Fowler, after twenty minutes of coaxing and beating, had had to come back another way. 'And I've never given in to a horse before, ma'am, believe me. But I'd be out there yet with that devil—' The same afternoon Christina had ridden through the gateway without any trouble.

'He takes to you, ma'am.' Christina found more comfort in

this fact than in anything else in her present life. When she rode out none of her problems loomed so large; there was a solace, and gleams of sunlight, optimism, the old quickening . . . almost happiness. 'Sorrow doesn't last for ever,' Christina thought, and was almost guilty.

But she was less supple than she used to be and knew that her riding days were numbered. Not that she could tell Fowler this.

'I think you'll have to turn him out in the park, and he can exercise himself,' she said.

'But he'll be clipped out in a day or two, ma'am.'

'Don't clip him, then.'

Fowler was aghast. But Christina would not listen to his protests. 'Everything is different now. You told me that yourself. It goes for the horses as well. There is a war on.'

Apart from the occasional aircraft overhead, which turned her heart over, it was hard at times to remember this fact. From a life that had been lived entirely for Will's leaves, scanning the newspapers daily for news of his squadron, personally involved in every fluctuation in the fortunes of the British Army, Christina found it hard to believe that, with Will's death, the war had not ended. Death was no nearer now than a clean-picked carcass left by a fox, or the rabbit in a poacher's snare.

'Can I have a ride on Pheasan' today?' Tizzy appeared at the door, as if drawn by talk of the horse. After the first few days he had swopped his allegiance from the cart-horses to Pheasant, drawn unerringly to the best horse in the stable. He had demanded to own him, but Christina would not give away this possession so easily. She had promised him a pony of his own, but he didn't want a pony. He wanted a horse. Christina remembered that she was going to try to find Woodpigeon, and promised him Woodpigeon, but Tizzy wanted Pheasant.

'You and your Pheasant!' Fowler grinned.

'He's *her* Pheasan',' Tizzy growled. 'She won' give 'im to me!'

'No, indeed! She gave you Marigold, didn't she?'

'I wan' Pheasan', too.'

'You've got more than you deserve already, young fellow-me-lad,' said Mary.

'Had he?' Christina wondered. He had transplanted well enough, but only to satisfy a stranger's whim; who was to say he would be happier at Flambards than in the rough and tumble of the brewery yard in Rotherhithe? Sometimes there was a look of bewilderment on his face, as if he didn't quite believe anything. He did not like his lonely bed at night and asked for his sisters, Iris and Amy, or whether he could come in with Christina, but Christina decided firmly that he would have to make do with Marigold. So he got Marigold in with him under the blankets, and talked to her in the dark. 'She keeps them old foxes off,' he said. Christina would not take the masks down, although in her heart she knew it would be kinder. But Tizzy was Mark's son, and not to be pandered to like a girl. He would have to live with the foxes; it was a part of his inheritence.

Chapter 6

Christina tried to convince herself that meeting Dick again was merely a business transaction, but when she actually alighted from the cab outside the Red Lion she was as nervous as the day she had knocked on Violet's door. The arrival of the steam ploughs at Flambards had spurred her to action. Shortly the land would be ready for drilling. The shining blades of the steam ploughs smashing through the virgin grass were merely the preliminary to the enterprise and when they left everything was going to be in her hands. She could not put off the problem of getting more labour any longer. If it was not Dick, it was going to be prisoners, in spite of what everybody said.

Having arrived at the Red Lion, she realized at once that she could not go into the public house on her own. Tizzy had assured her that the pub was Dick's day-time haunt—not in itself a good omen—so she was fairly sure of finding him. But it had not occurred to her, until faced with the door of the tap-room, that she could hardly enter such a strange place without an escort.

She turned and called to the cabbie, who was gathering up his reins.

'Just a moment!'

He looked fairly affable, a rather portly middle-aged man with a black moustache.

'Could you do something for me?'

'Anything for a lady,' he said gallantly.

'Will you take me into the saloon and buy me a drink? I'm looking for someone, and I don't like to go in alone.'

'It'll be a pleasure, ma'am.' He beamed down on her, unhooking his apron. 'It's not every day a drink comes in the line of duty, as you might say.'

Christina waited while he hitched on the horse's nosebag. When she had dressed she had considered herself, as on the previous expedition, inconspicuous rather than smart, but now she felt positively flamboyant. Even her dullest clothes were far more Hendon than Rotherhithe. She gave the cabbie a shilling and said, 'A small port, please. And whatever you wish. I'm very grateful.'

He opened the door for her with a cheerful bow, and she went in, trying to be casual. The bar was warm and fairly full, and the conversation loud, but nothing came to a stop when she entered; a few curious glances flicked her, but merely in passing. She slipped into a place at a table and let out a sigh of relief.

'A small port, m'm?' The cabbie turned the shilling over in his hand.

'Yes, and ask if Dick Wright is in here, will you?' She was amazed how cool she sounded, asking for Dick. But now it was done the panic subsided; a sense of the inevitable took its place, as it had before. Christina knew that she was no longer in charge of the situation. She sat very still, satisfactorily anonymous in this urban atmosphere, taking in the vulgar comfort of the leather-buttoned settles and marble-topped tables, the big fire burning in the polished grate and the lights reflected in the engraved mirrors that stretched up to the ceiling. It seemed very obvious that Dick should prefer the Red Lion to the bare provision of Violet's sitting-room.

When Dick came Christina realized that she had been expecting him to be just the same, as if no war, no violence had touched him. She had forgotten her original opinion when Dick had joined the Army, that Dick's whole nature, his kindness, his slow, considered ways and sensitivity towards other people's—even horses'—feelings, was the very antithesis of all the Army stood for. She remembered it now.

He came up slowly, and she watched him coming, and could find no words, easy words, to say. He looked ill. Where she remembered him brown, almost ruddy, he was now very pale, so that the golden-fair hair—which had not changed—made no contrast at all. He also looked—and Christina knew the word was novelettish, but it was the only one that fitted—haunted. His eyes, always rather cautious, were withdrawn with what Christina could only recognize as pain, but whether physical or spiritual she could not tell. His face was thin and drawn, and the unfamiliar, cheap suit he wore hung on his once stocky frame; the big brown hands, that had soothed so many horses (and, once, herself) were white and unmarked—ill hands. Christina looked up at him and tried to keep the shock out of her face. Only, with Dick, who was completely honest, one did not cover up for long.

'Dick, may I talk to you?' She spoke quietly, very matter-of-fact, to squash her emotions.

'Yes, ma'am.'

He had a half-filled glass of bitter in his hand which he set down on the table. Christina had her port, and the cab-driver, having produced Dick, melted away into the crush round the bar. Dick sat down. He looked at Christina without embarrassment, his expression very guarded.

'I came to see if you would come back to Flambards to work?'

Although Dick did not move, Christina felt as if he had flinched. And with the mention of Flambards came—to Christina as well as, she knew, to Dick—a swift vision of everything that had once happened there, so that it was as if the smell of beer and the fuggy, tobacco-laden atmosphere did not exist; it was replaced by the smell of horses' sweat and the damp wood where once Sweetbriar and Woodpigeon had walked side by side. Christina looked at Dick, stricken.

'Oh, Dick, are you all right? What happened to you? When Tizzy said . . .' And the mention of Tizzy did nothing to restore her calm, for she knew that, in taking him away, she had behaved as she always had towards this struggling family, using them to further her own interests. Even the offer of a job to Dick . . . She was ashamed. The colour came up into her cheeks. 'Dick, I'm sorry if . . .' She was sorry for more than there were words to say it, how sadly awry all their plans had worked out. She shook her head. She was lost.

'Is Tizzy happy?' Dick said.

She nodded.

Dick was silent, staring down into his bitter.

Christina, unable to bear the silence, explained: 'We've got eight horses to keep—six cart-horses . . . there's only Fowler to look after them. The land is all being ploughed up, but we're dreadfully short of labour. I thought—' Her voice trailed away.

She made a great effort to pull herself together, and said, 'I would like you to come.'

Dick said slowly, 'I can't take a job, Miss Christina. I'm not fit for anything.'

'Why, what has happened?'

'I was discharged with T.B.'

'But you're better now!' Christina, with sudden vehemence, could not accept that Dick could be threatened by this terrible disease. 'You must be, else you'd be in a sanitorium!'

'I came out of hospital six months ago.'

'How long were you in? How did you get it?'

'A shell splinter through the lung, at Ypres.' He shrugged. 'I'm alive, at least. I was sorry when Violet said about Mr. William.'

He did not mention Mark. Everything that had happened between the four of them touched Christina again, and withered. The war had blasted them all.

'But what will you do?'

'I've got a pension for the time being, and there's Vi's place. I'm all right.'

He looked less all right than anyone Christina had seen for a long time. But his old manner, reserved, guarded, held Christina's concern at bay. Perhaps because he saw her feelings, he gave a sudden smile and said, 'The poaching's not much good in Rotherhithe, that's the only trouble.'

Christina smiled shakily. 'No trout in the Thames?'

He shook his head.

Desperately, because there was nothing else to say, Christina said, 'When you get better, in the spring, will you come? You'd improve quicker in the fresh air—that's what they say for chests, surely?' She could hardly tell him that she wanted him to come just because he was Dick, and someone she could talk to, and ask advice of, even depend on. She felt now that she wanted someone for that even more than someone to plough and drill and harrow.

'I can't promise anything, Miss Christina. I'll come if it's—' He hesitated. 'If it's right.' 'Right' covered a multitude of conditions, more subtle than Christina could divine. She knew that the visit was a failure. All she had done was to dredge up feelings best left undisturbed, and sadden herself by revealing possibilities that were not to be. The visit, as on the last occasion they had met, had probably not done Dick any good either. 'I learn nothing,' Christina thought. She told him about Pheasant, and how Fowler and Mary were, all the things it was safe to talk about, but not about Will or Mark or Tizzy. The safe subjects were so limited that, presently, she got up and said, 'I must go back.'

Dick came to the tram stop with her, hunched against the cold wind, in spite of her protest. It seemed strange to be with him in the ugly, urban setting. Dick must have sensed the same thing, for he lifted his head to a gleam of sunlight and the wild, ragged clouds over the river and said, 'Good hunting weather.' Christina could not bring herself to say anything.

Some days later the gang with the steam ploughs left Flambards, and Christina rode Pepper round the farm. Acre upon acre of turned earth stretched in every direction, gleaming in the rain. It was the wettest autumn anyone could remember. The choked ditches spilled their overflow into the new plough till it was striped with reflected sky, and the tracks were rivers and the ponds lakes. The moorhens and the mallards swam across the lawn of the empty farm-house; the foxes, their earths flooded, howled in the dusk and ran out of the coverts, heading for higher land.

'I shall never make anything of it,' Christina thought, appalled by her task. Nobody else cared, not even Fowler. Only that they got their pay and a square meal inside them. Stanley was taking oats home for his father's cob and Harry, solemnly teaching Tizzy how to lay a hedge, himself laid a few yards an hour, working with intense concentration. Christina remembered how one autumn, when Mark was seventeen, he had cut and laid the whole length of the park hedge in one day.

December came. Drilling would be impossible until the spring, Mr. Masters said. He couldn't remember anything like it since he came to Mickleditch. 'Nineteen sixteen, hurry and go,' Christina said, looking out over the tangled, sodden garden from her bedroom window. 'You have been no good to me.' She was too awkward to ride any more, and no longer wanted to see the waiting plough. Christmas meant nothing, nor any time beyond.

Chapter 7

'We'll turn your new pony out with Pheasant and Wood-pigeon,' Christina said to Tizzy, 'so that he'll exercise himself if you don't ride him. And he'll be no extra work for Fowler.'

'When can I ride Pheasan'?'

'You won't be riding Pheasant. What do you think we bought you a pony of your own for? Pheasant is mine. I shall be riding him again soon.'

'You're too fat to ride.'

'I shan't always be as fat as this. What are you going to call your pony?'

'Worm.'

'*Worm?* You can't call him Worm! It's a horrible name.'

'Well, Pheasan's the same colour as a pheasan' an' Worm's the same colour as a worm.'

Christina laughed, in spite of her exasperation. It was true.

The little Welsh pony was a strawberry-roan, not pure chestnut and white as old Sweetbriar had been, but more a mixture of grey and bay. He was a stocky, bold pony with a pretty head and a mass of grey forelock over his quick eyes. Christina secretly thought he would be more than enough for Tizzy to handle, but Tizzy, to her bitter disappointment, had not shown any excitement over his Christmas present. 'He's too li'le,' he said. 'I wan' Pheasan'. Or a Shire horse.'

'Well, I'm not going to call him Worm,' she said firmly. 'It's not fair on him to have a horrid name.'

'He likes it,' Tizzy said. 'He wan's to be called Worm. Like I wan'ed to be called Tizzy.'

Christina had tried to call Tizzy Thomas, but he had resolutely refused to answer to it, even after several bangs from a furious Mary.

'I'm Tizzy. Tizzy Bugg.' It was true that his unfortunate surname was Bugg, but Christina was having it changed in the legal papers to Russell. 'Tizzy Bugg on Worm,' she thought, and laughed. Tizzy looked up at her stubbornly, his underlip pushed out.

'What you laughin' for?'

'Worm.'

'It's not a funny name,' Tizzy said furiously. 'It's a good name. He *likes* it.'

'All right. Worm.' But in her mind she refused to call the pony Worm.

They let the little gelding go, and hung over the gate watching Pheasant and Woodpigeon cropping the yellow winter grass. Fowler had gone to buy Woodpigeon off the doctor, having to pay what he thought was a prodigious sum in order to tempt the man to sell. Woodpigeon had been, apparently, an exemplary doctor's gig-horse just as, in his earlier days, he had been an exemplary lady's hunter. Christina did not regret the money; Woodpigeon was a part of Flambards, the only survivor of the old horses, as she was the only survivor of the people. He was snow-white now. Both the horses were unclipped, covered in mud. Fowler, even now, never stopped shaking his head over their appearance. But all he had to do was bring them in at night and turn them out in the morning, and feed them. It was all he had time for. He had six cart-horses to look after and spent most of his time over at the farm, bullying Stanley, who could not be trusted to do the horses properly without supervision. There was a yard of bullocks to be fed, too. When the animals were comfortable, Fowler worked on the rusty machinery, oiling and sharpening and renewing bolts and fittings. But who was going to use the machinery when it was all in working order, Christina had yet to discover.

'Come on.' She held a hand out to Tizzy. 'Let's go and get our tea. Mary should have it ready now.'

'There's a man coming,' Tizzy said. 'On a bike.'

It was true, to Christina's surprise. She rarely had visitors, for her action in bringing Tizzy back to Flambards had so shocked the neighbourhood that few people could bring themselves to call. Christina did not care, for she was used to facing her problems alone, but she could not honestly admit that she was not hurt, and certainly she was astonished by the attitude. Having lived for so long amongst Will's crowd, she had forgotten how narrow-minded a small country village could be. Tizzy himself, so remarkably like his father, could not be passed off as any stray orphan, even had Christina wished it, and Christina realized that his history was known to every busybody in the parish. Only Mrs. Masters, straightforward and realistic, came to see Christina; it was through her that Christina learned how much gossip she had provoked. 'But I wouldn't let it worry you, my dear,' Mrs. Masters said. 'They've nothing else to think about, that's their trouble. And in a few years it will all be forgotten—there'll be some new scandal . . . that's how it is in a little place like this.' And Christina, who had come to love Tizzy more than she sometimes thought was wise, was comforted.

They waited for the man on the bicycle, curious. He dismounted in a stately fashion, raised his cap, and said, 'Mrs. Russell? I'm from the Essex Agricultural War Association. About your application for prisoners of war—'

Christina looked at him eagerly. 'Oh, yes! I was hoping to hear from you. Is it all right? Can you send me—'

'One hand, ma'am, as from next Monday morning. The truck will drop him here at seven in the morning and pick him up at seven in the evening.'

'One! Only one?'

'Yes, ma'am. We haven't got all that many available, just at the moment.'

Christina was bitterly disappointed. 'I want a dozen! What good is one? Oh, if only you knew—'

'Yes, it's the same all over, ma'am, I'm afraid.' The official was very official, standing beside his bicycle. Christina, her heart having leapt with anticipation, was dashed. She could have wept with frustration. The man rode away.

'Are we havin' a *Hun*?' Tizzy asked, with relish.

'Yes.'

'I'll shoot him.'

'I'll shoot *you*.'

'Stanley says if we have Huns he'll knock their teeth in.'

'If Stanley wants to knock Huns about, he can enlist,' Christina said crisply. 'I'll have a word with him.'

No farm, she thought, could have a more motley gang of workers than hers. Even herself . . . for a farmer she was a strange shape. Dr. Porter said the child would be born at the beginning of March, in another three weeks. Christina would gladly have passed her days merely eating and sleeping. She was glad to get indoors and sit by the cheerful log fire in her sitting-room—one of the very few plans concerning Flambards that had turned out successfully. The little gold sitting-room was her lair, her own private place where Mary and Fowler couldn't get at her (save by discreetly knocking), where she could curl up on the sofa and watch Tizzy marching his lead soldiers (once his father's) across the hearthrug, shoving Marigold's sprawl out of the way. This was where she felt she had the beginning of a home . . . Tizzy marched his lead soldiers up over Marigold's warm, pale flank—'Over the top,' he said, and Marigold growled softly in her sleep—and Christina felt the strange, anonymous stirrings inside her of the child Will had so surprisingly left, and thought how little she knew of what comprised both birth and death. She knew of nobody near to her who had had a baby. She knew it wasn't particularly constructive to lie and think about the baby, when there were the ledgers to do and farming manuals to learn from, but it was all she really wanted to do, all the time, just dream. And her dreams were more hopeful now. 'It is improving,' she thought, very careful in what she allowed her mind to dwell on. In the pretty bureau

71

by the window all Will's letters and the photographs were locked away, and she had not looked at them for six months.

'This Hun,' Tizzy said, 'p'raps he drove a Zepp'lin?'

Tizzy was fascinated by Zeppelins, having once seen one in a searchlight over the Thames. From Flambards on a clear still night he could see distant searchlights weaving over the river to the south, and would stand on the window-sill, pressed avidly against the glass.

'Perhaps.'

When the prisoner arrived Tizzy had obviously forgotten all about shooting him, for he ran to meet him to find out if he had 'driven a Zeppelin'. Christina, huddled in a thick shawl, went out into the icy, dark morning, hoping to see a strapping young Prussian striding up the drive, but instead she found a small, gentle-faced, middle-aged man nervously waiting for orders. He looked so cold and ill and worn that Christina's heart plummeted yet again, and, because he was so much older than herself, she was at a loss suddenly, unable to give him orders. She did not know what to say.

'What is your name?' she asked helplessly.

But the man looked puzzled, and said something in German.

'Name?' Christina said again. 'Fritz? Er—Hans—' She couldn't think of any more.

'Wilhelm.'

Christina shivered, unable to help herself. She felt utterly dejected all over again, her disappointment flooding up. She told Tizzy to take the man to Fowler in the stable-yard, and turned indoors.

But Wilhelm, amazingly, was a farmer by trade, and when Fowler took him to the stables the German picked the best pair of horses without hesitation and harnessed them to the drill. Fowler took a wagon out to the first field and unloaded the sacks of seed along the hedge, and Wilhelm filled the hopper and started to drill the first stretch, the horses moving for him with a willingness that proved they recognized a master hand. When Fowler came in for his lunch his face twitched with excitement.

'Why, ma'am, he uses them horses like my own father used to do! You won't get a better man than that anywhere, Fritz or no Fritz!'

'Wilhelm,' Tizzy said.

Christina's eyes glowed. The news was almost too good to be true.

'Most of 'em don't know one end of a turnip from the other, from what I've heard, let alone how to drill corn! You've done well, ma'am! Dang me, I couldn't believe my eyes when I saw him go up that field!'

'Perhaps we'll have something to harvest this year after all!'

Wilhelm ate outside with Stanley and Harry. Christina saw

little of him, for she was too heavy to want to be seen about much; she went for walks through the covert with Marigold, where she knew she was on her own, and found a marvellous content with glimpses of her newly drilled fields from the edge of the trees. The land was drying out, and golden clumps of primroses were pushing up on the banks, their starred faces opening to the first soft hint of spring. Christina was full of optimism. 'It is beginning,' she thought, and there was a warmth in the air that went with her mood. 'It is going to be all right.' Marigold crashed through the undergrowth, her pink tongue grinning. 'Soon I shall be able to ride again,' Christina thought, and she quickened with excitement. 'And the *child*! Soon . . .' and she was so grateful for having something to look forward to that she could not help sniffing with pure sentiment.

Four days later Christina, after a very restless night, decided it was time to send for Dr. Porter. She had said nothing to Mary about how she felt, for she could not bear Mary's fuss, having had enough to put up with the last few weeks listening to the fantastic tales of childbirth that the old woman loved to tell. Of course, now that the moment had arrived, Christina was alone in the house. Mary had gone shopping and Tizzy was out in the fields. Christina fetched her coat and went down to the stables to find somebody.

It was lunch-time, and the boys were sitting in the hay-shed eating their bread and dripping. Harry was eating, at least, but Stanley, having finished, was doing a charade with a bale of hay and a pitchfork, charging across the yard with the pitchfork in front of him like a bayonet and 'stabbing' the hay with vicious glee, shouting, 'Take that, you dirty Hun! Achtung! Achtung! Swinehund!' The hay bale burst its strings, spilling its entrails into the March wind, and Stanley roared with laughter. 'You dirty, blubbering Boche!' Obscene epithets spat from his lips, and his face was filled with a malicious glee.

From his seat on the horse-trough, the German prisoner sat watching the performance. He had finished his handful of boiled potatoes and was hunched with his back to the wind, the collar of his tattered field-grey jacket turned up. His expression was one of utter sadness, not of anger; Christina had never seen a human being look more forlorn. She stood, astonished, her mission quite forgotten, and saw Harry's vacant laughter crumble as he caught sight of her. Stanley turned round and dropped the pitchfork, the animation clouding into truculence.

'Stanley!'

Christina's burning indignation was interrupted at the first breath by a pain so sharp as to remind her of what she had come for. She leaned back against the wall, furiously angry, but unable to say anything. Wilhelm got off the trough and came towards her, his face full of concern. Christina recovered herself, and saw Stanley smirking.

'Get on your bicycle and go and fetch Dr. Porter!' she said to him, her voice shaking. She was so angry she was nearly in tears. Wilhelm was talking to her in gentle, worried German.

'How dare he treat you like that!' Christina muttered. 'How dare he be—so—so—' She found she was trembling all over. She felt very strange.

Wilhelm took her back to the house, holding her arm. She sat in the chair by the kitchen fire and he made her a cup of tea, still talking in his anxious German. Every so often he made mimes, pointing upstairs, making a sleeping face, eyes shut, to suggest she should go to bed. He held up six fingers, pointing to himself with a shy smile. 'Kinder,' he said, tapping his chest, waving his fingers. He scrabbled in the pocket of his threadbare uniform and showed her a tattered, almost indecipherable photograph of a fat, smiling woman surrounded by children. 'Mein frau,' he said. He filled a hot-water bottle and pointed upstairs again.

'How strange,' Christina thought, not much caring any more, 'if my baby is delivered by a German prisoner!'

But presently Mary arrived, a torrent of consternation, and Christina lost track. People came and went and she lay in bed and watched Dr. Porter sitting by the fire, reading *The Times*. She thought of Tizzy, and Pheasant. 'So this is what it's like,' she said to herself, amazed. It went on and on. 'Germans Evacuate Bapaume,' Christina read, across the room. 'Many casualties.' Dr. Porter bent down and put another piece of coal on the fire, and leaned back, legs crossed, thumbs in his waistcoat pocket. He shut his eyes and dozed. 'How stupid men are!' Christina thought. It got dark and Mary brought the lamps. Christina saw the lights dancing, doubled up and multiplied across the ceiling as if the house were on fire. Dr. Porter had got up at last and she saw his face over her, with big shadows for eyes. The child was born at midnight.

'It's a girl,' Dr. Porter said.

They bathed it and gave it to her, and out of the shawls Christina saw two black eyes squinting with bewilderment, the reflections of the lamps flickering in them, and a tuft of black hair. She gazed and gazed at it, at the wandering, puzzled eyes, and was carried away on what felt like—no, it is impossible, she thought. Impossible to be so happy. But she was. She had never felt anything like it in all her life. She lay with the baby in her arms, and let this miraculous content lap her, hardly daring to believe in anything.

Mary, with her exceptional talent for saying the wrong thing, dabbed her eyes and said, 'And to think I did the same thing for the first Mrs. Russell, in this very room, twenty-two years ago! And the baby then was this little darling's own father! I remember——'

'Go away,' Christina said. 'Leave me alone. I want to sleep.' It wasn't true. She just didn't want her happiness shattered. They left her and she lay awake until the sky started to go light over the covert and then she slept.

Tizzy came to see her at lunch-time, carrying a dish of rice pudding. He prodded the baby curiously.

'What you goin' to call it?'

'I don't know. What names do you like?'

'Boxer's nice. Or Ginger.'

'It's not a horse.'

'Marigol' then.'

'We'd get muddled, with two Marigolds.'

'Can Marigol' have a puppy? Can' you tell her to have one?'

'Well—perhaps.' It was a good idea. 'Yes. We must find her a good husband.'

'Who's your husband? Fowler?'

Christina giggled.

'Oh, ma'am! He needs a good hiding!' Mary said. 'The things he comes out with.'

Tizzy climbed on to the bed and flung his arms round Christina. He smelt of hay and earth and horses, and Christina hugged him. 'I don' wan' a good hiding,' he muttered into her hair. '*She* wan's a good hiding. I don' like that baby. What you

76

wan' it for? It's not as good as Pheasan'. I'd rather have Pheasan' any day.'

'Yes. Pheasant's lovely. The baby'll be all right when it's older. You'll like her then.'

'It's not much good now.'

'No.'

'Why can' we call it Boxer?'

Christina did not waste much time in bed. The baby was strong and healthy and contented, but the ill-assorted farm-labourers were wasting precious time, larking about in the fields. Fowler looked after the horses, but would do nothing else—indeed, moving between the two stable-yards, he had little time to do anything else, so that Stanley and Harry were left un-supervised. They had their jobs to do, but whether they did them was doubtful. The bullocks looked poor even to Christina's inexperienced eyes; she dare not buy milking-cows until she could rely on someone to milk them. Wilhelm knew how to cultivate the fields, but could hardly be expected to do the work without any orders. Even those he was given, he did not under-stand. Christina's happiness was short-lived.

'I must have been mad,' she thought, staring out of her bed-room window. Everything was growing fast. The covert was a tangle of new green, the rooks and the starlings spinning against the dawn sky, the garden thrusting, unquenched, below, even the rosebuds growing, tight and mossy, out of the gnarled maze of the bushes. And beyond the covert the corn was showing in perfect, precise lines, not a furrow missed or doubled, not a headland neglected. The first hay crop would soon be ready to take. But Christina, instead of being proud and excited, was terrified by her responsibilities. There was only her to decide when to start cutting the hay, when to roll and harrow. No one else cared. Mr. Masters and one or two neighbouring farmers had given her advice in passing, but all had too much to do on their own farms to bother much with her; she knew from the way they spoke that they both despised and pitied her for presuming to do a man's job. And if her corn grew, she did not see how she could possibly cope with a harvest.

'I wanted it to grow,' she said to the morning air, 'and now it is growing I'm more worried than ever.'

Suppose it hadn't grown, she thought? Suppose the baby had had a hare lip, or a crooked leg? But her corn was growing and her baby smiled at her, and she still worried. 'I am so stupid.' She plaited her hair into one long, thick pigtail, and went to the cot by the bed and lifted out the baby.

'My little Isobel, your mother is so stupid it's not true.'

She had called the child after Will's mother, not being able to find any female equivalent of William that was bearable. The baby was warm and wet and utterly adorable. She made Christina want to laugh and cry at the same time. But as she sat and nursed her she was thinking of the farm.

When she went down to the stable she found Fowler gibbering with frustration. Wilhelm, having been asked to fetch a load of hay up to the stables, had fetched straw. He stood by, uncomprehending, while Fowler cursed him. His sad, peasant face with the ragged greying moustache turned to Christina, puzzled, appealing, but Christina could not comfort him, for she knew no German. She told Fowler to be quiet, and conveyed to Wilhelm with vigorous mime what was wrong, and watched him turn the wagon round and start trudging back to the farm. His dejection depressed her in turn. It was another failure, that she could not even reward her best worker save by making more work for him.

'He does his best,' she said to Fowler. 'You shouldn't shout at him.'

The sound of an aeroplane engine made them both glance up. It was not an unfamiliar noise these days, for there was an airfield quite close by.

'I like to see them machines about these days,' Fowler said. 'What with those Gothas the Germans are sending over.'

The machine was a BE12; Christina registered the fact automatically. She had learned to accept now that aeroplanes still flew, although Will was no longer alive to fly them; she could watch them without her expression changing.

'A person isn't safe in his own home any more,' Fowler complained. 'I never thought I'd live to see such a thing.'

Christina didn't say anything. German bombers were the least of her troubles, although they had passed very close on more than one occasion, following the rivers towards London. The thumping of the A.A. guns had sent the rooks wheeling in alarm, and old Mary diving under the kitchen table. Tizzy had leapt with excitement.

Back at the house Mary said, 'There's a letter come for you, ma'am,' and Christina took it from her curiously. Most of her letters were solicitors' letters or bills, or from Aunt Grace, but this one was from France, in an unfamiliar writing. She opened it and looked at the signature first. It was from Dorothy, the daughter of her old employer, the girl who had shared the excitements of the flying days before the war had turned flying into something quite different. Christina read it avidly, touched by the old relationship.

Dorothy was nursing in France, and was writing because she had heard about Christina's child. 'How lovely for you! I am terribly happy, after all your heartbreak. I would love to come and see you again when I get leave. There is nowhere to go now. The hotel is full of convalescing officers and Father let the house —it seemed pointless to keep it on. I cannot tell you everything that has happened. We work here until we fall asleep on our feet. You could not imagine the things I have learnt to take for granted! I have heard nothing from Mark and suppose there is no hope now? I last got a note from Seddülbahir, but the fighting there was said to be terrible. I have wept over so many people, sometimes I think it is all just a nightmare, but I am not the only one.'

Christina's memories were stirred up by the letter. That Dorothy, the girl who had everything, had taken on one of the most appalling jobs of the war impressed her, and made her even more impatient with her own attempts to do anything useful. She stood at the window of her sitting-room, the letter in her hands, looking out over the grazed park. 'If only I can make it work, this place!' Dorothy's grit strengthened her. 'I could get milking-cows and milk them myself, if there's no one else . . .' Dorothy, surely, was doing more than milk cows? Dorothy, of all people, the girl who could turn any man's head, who could fly an aeroplane, who had worn the smartest clothes in London . . . Christina was seized with a great restlessness. She nursed the baby, but her thoughts were all over the place and Isobel cried, her face crumpling into red rage, her little fists flailing.

'Oh, my little cross-patch, my little scarecrow! Are you so angry? Is it all my fault?' She sat the little hiccuping bundle on her knee and was rewarded with a wavering smile. The great dark eyes—Mark's, Will's, Tizzy's, and now Isobel's—regarded her with the habitual curiosity.

'You bad-tempered little Russell!' Christina murmured, charmed and soothed. 'You little bossy baby.'

Isobel laughed.

But later, when Mary had pushed the baby out in her perambulator—which she loved to do—Christina was still restless. Tizzy was away with Wilhelm. Another aeroplane whined in the sky. It was warm, June; the sun was hot. A swallow had built a nest in the porch by the front door and swooped in and out, endlessly busy. There was a smell of strawberries from the kitchen and grass and dust from outside: everything, in nature, that ordinarily made up happiness, but Christina could only remember that it was just a year since Will died. The swallows and the strawberries . . . it all went on just the same, and so did she, but . . . 'But what?' she said to herself. She went and stood in the shade of the porch, her cheek against the cold ivy leaves. It was as if her very feelings had died, sometimes. 'I was all right,' she thought, 'until I read Dorothy's letter, and it reminded me.' It was very quiet and hot and still. Christina did not hear anything, leaning against the wall of the house, until a voice said, hesitantly, 'Miss Christina.'

She turned, and saw Dick standing watching her.

She straightened up. There was no sense of shock, not even of surprise, only an uncanny sense of things happening that were quite inevitable, almost as if she had been waiting for Dick.

'Dick! Oh, Dick, I'm glad you've come.' Even her voice did not sound surprised.

Dick looked at her rather anxiously. 'Are you all right, ma'am?'

'Yes, of course I am! What about you? Oh, it's so hot! You must be worn out. Come into the kitchen and I'll get you a drink. Have you come from London?'

'Yes, ma'am.'

Christina felt as if she was waking up. It was almost as if Dick had appeared in a dream and, now that she was coming to, he was still in front of her. She led the way into the house, across the flagged hall and down the passage into the kitchen.

The kitchen doors were open and the strawberry basket was on the table where Mary had left it. Christina fetched Dick a glass of beer from the barrel that was kept for the men.

'Sit down. Have you eaten? There's some pie left in the pantry if you're hungry.'

'No, thank you, ma'am. The beer'll do me nicely.'

Christina watched Dick as he drank. He looked better than when she had seen him in Rotherhithe, but was still thin and frail-looking compared with the old Dick. She could not keep the anxiety out of her face.

'Are you better now?'

'Better than I was, ma'am.'

'You will stay?'

Dick said in a low voice, 'I couldn't turn down your offer, Miss Christina. But I'm no worker, not any more. I'll earn my keep, that's all I ask.'

'But, Dick, the boys will do the heavy work. If you just watch them, and decide what's to be done, and run the place as it should be run, then you'll be worth all the gold in the world! You see, I don't *know*.'

'Well, horses are my trade, ma'am. I'm no farmer. But my father was first horseman on this farm all his life for old Mr. Russell, and I worked with him ever since I could walk, so I know the work. I was brought up with it, until I got promoted to the hunters as a stable-boy, with a wage of my own. So I dare say I could tell you what needs doing and suchlike, even if I couldn't do it.' He paused. 'I've thought about it; I couldn't stop thinking about it, ever since you came. But I don't know if it's right now.'

'Oh, it is!' Christina said fervently. 'It must be! You don't know how badly we can do with you here!'

'I reckoned I could feed stock, and milk cows, do a bit of thatching and that. Enough to earn my meals. But if it's no good, then I won't stay.'

Christina leaned on the table, and felt the emotion catching up with her. She did not show anything to Dick, but she felt as if she had been plucked up by a surging flood of good fortune: the very thing she had most wished for had happened. She felt almost dizzy with it. She had to be very careful to show that she was not as demented as, at that moment, she felt. She straightened up and said, very casually, 'Would you like to come and have a look round? We'll go and see Fowler.'

'Very well, ma'am.'

He picked up his cap and they walked out through the side door into the drive. Nothing was said as they passed under the deep shade of the chestnut-trees and through the gates into the stable-yard. Christina was careful not to remember anything, only think of the welfare of her farm, and how it would thrive with Dick's sense behind it. Only when Fowler caught sight of Dick did she burst out laughing, because of his expression.

He dropped the bale of hay he had just taken from Wilhelm and stared. 'Why, dang me! If it isn't— God 'strewth, Dick, my lad! My old boy, Dick!' He came up, his hand held out, his cheeks bright red with excitement. 'What they been doing to you, then, boy? You don't look like the same Dick as left here, not by a long chalk. 'Strewth, Dick, you want to get some flesh on you before you drop down the drainhole here.'

They all laughed again, even Dick. Wilhelm, standing by the fresh load of hay, watched them, puzzled. Then, as Fowler went on chatting to Dick, he came up to Christina and asked her something incomprehensible, pointing to the hayload. Christina scratched her head. 'Oh, I don't know!' But Dick turned round and said something to Wilhelm in German, and Wilhelm's face lit up. He gabbled to Dick, the words tumbling out, his moustache quivering with relief. And Dick nodded, and said to Fowler, 'Do you want any more hay, he wants to know?'

'No, I don't, and if you can talk to that Hun I reckon you're worth your keep more than the rest of us on this farm put together, eh, Miss Christina?'

Christina's relief was almost as great as Wilhelm's.

'He's by far the best worker we've got,' she said to Dick, 'only we can never tell him what we want. It's ridiculous.'

She felt positively light-hearted. Fowler was chuckling, clapping Wilhelm on the shoulder and saying, 'We'll get through to you yet, old thickhead.'

'We'll go down to the farm in the wagon,' Christina decided. 'Wilhelm's got to take it back. It'll save us a walk.'

'Very well, ma'am.'

Wilhelm drove the wagon and Christina and Dick sat on the side boards. Christina watched the breeze lifting the hayseeds into small eddies round her feet, and wondered if it was right to feel so optimistic, when half an hour ago she had been so miserable. Feeling happy, after all this time, disturbed her. She felt almost ashamed, guilty, of being happy. 'But it's a year,' she thought. She felt her hair blowing out from its untidy coil and the sun hot on her face.

When they got down to the farm they found Stanley still working on the stable roof, with Tizzy perched up beside him.

'Tizzy!' Christina shouted up to him. 'Look who's here!'

Tizzy stood up on the sloping, exposed rafters. Christina saw him against the sky, his little brown figure balanced without fear, his expression uncertain.

'It's Uncle Dick!' Christina shouted.

But Tizzy went on standing there, his underlip stuck out, looking very much as he had the first time Christina had set eyes on him.

'I don' wan'—'

'Come down!' Christina shouted sharply. She was hurt, for Dick's sake, by Tizzy's reluctance. But Dick was smiling. He jumped down from the cart.

'Come on, you little don' wanter! I'm not going to take you away!'

'I'm not goin' away!' Tizzy shouted. 'I'm not! I'm not—' His eyes sparked beneath his forelock of tangled hair. Christina stood up in the cart and shouted, 'Come down, you idiot child! Nobody's going to take you away. You belong here. Uncle Dick's come to stay!'

And Tizzy came, sliding down the thatch on the seat of his breeches. Christina jumped down and went to join them. Tizzy's face was now all smiles, and so was Dick's. 'Why,' Christina thought, 'it's like a family!' And the thought gave her the strangest of all the shocks she had received that day.

Chapter 8

It was arranged that Dick should live in the old farm-house. He was not concerned over its condition, but Christina went in herself and cleaned it out. Dick said he would use only the kitchen, which was a large room with a door leading directly into the stable-yard, so Christina hung curtains at the windows and got Wilhelm to transport a few pieces of furniture over from Flambards in the wagon, so that the place had a bed, a table and a chair, and mats on the floor. 'Why, it's a palace!' Dick said. 'You shouldn't have gone to all that trouble, ma'am.' And Christina, remembering Violet's living-room, supposed that it was, by comparison.

Christina sent plenty of food down to the farm, with whoever was going, determined to build up Dick's strength. As she had foreseen, Dick's arrival changed the whole tenor of life at Flambards: Stanley immediately started to work, Harry seemed to gather his wits together, Wilhelm became more cheerful, and Fowler stopped grumbling. Christina, for the first time since she had come to Flambards, began to think that the miracle might actually happen: that there would be a harvest at the end of the summer. Already the hay was being cut, and Christina went up each lunch-time with the beer, and stayed to help. Tizzy was in his element with Uncle Dick in charge; he worked all day long leading the wagons to the stack and taking the empty ones back, and grew as brown as a gipsy. When he came home with Wilhelm in the evenings he would be furry with hay-dust, his eyes red-rimmed. 'Come on, my little hedgehog.' Christina would get his supper, and hope he stayed awake long enough to eat it. Even the baby's face was brown under her cotton bonnet. Mary pushed her up to the fields to watch the horses, and generally put up a few haycocks herself when the reaper came near her. 'It's a real farm,' Christina thought, watching. Even Marigold, panting in the shade of a wagon, was part of it. She was in whelp to an elderly foxhound Fowler had found pensioned off with a farmer a few miles away, one of the original Flambards hounds. 'There's the beginning of a new pack there,' Fowler would say, 'come the end of the war, and things are right again.' Tizzy looked after her with solicitude, even bringing a bowl from the kitchen 'for her beer' at lunch-time.

And Dick, if he grew no fatter, at least lost his Rotherhithe pallor and became the colour that Christina remembered him. He did none of the heavy work, as he had promised, and would only take five shillings for wages—'If I take more, I shall do more; then it might all come to more harm than good,' he said, so Christina did not press him. But his presence resulted in more work being produced by Stanley and Harry than Christina had dreamed was possible, and the haystacks, built under his direction, were as perfect as Mr. Masters's, as symmetrical as flower-pots. Christina could stand and gaze at them for minutes on end, entirely absorbed by their beauty. Dick thatched them himself, with Stanley to fetch up the straw. It was hot, and the men worked without shirts, and on Dick's back Christina saw the ugly sprawling scar that was his legacy from Ypres; Stanley saw it, too, and made no more jokes about bashing up the Huns. He had received his calling-up papers, and asked Christina if she would plead his case before the tribunal, on the grounds that he was doing essential work.

'You do essential work if someone's watching you,' she said to him rather bitterly, 'but you don't if there's no one to keep you at it.'

'Please, ma'am, you won't be sorry, I promise you.' Stanley licked his lips nervously. Christina, despising him, agreed to

85

see what she could do. Dick said, 'If you just keep him until after the harvest, it'll be something gained.' So Stanley got his deferment for a further six months. At the same tribunal the youngest Masters boy was also exempted. Christina, saddened by the world's injustice, drove herself home and reported to Dick. He smiled at her indignation. 'People only do what's in their nature,' he said, as if it were very simple. 'There's no one to blame.'

'But it's not fair!'

'It's as fair as they can make it.' There was a pause, and he added, 'Ma'am.'

'Don't call me ma'am,' Christina said, irritated by its irrelevance. Dick said nothing.

'Come over and have supper. I'll take you and Tizzy back together,' Christina said. She had come straight over to the farm with Pepper in the dog-cart to report the tribunal's decision, and could see that Dick was finished for the day, and was about to retire to his kitchen to make his own supper.

'Mary's made rabbit pie,' she added. Dick, who usually had his shot-gun handy, kept the kitchen well supplied. Christina had yet to see him miss anything he fired at, and presumed— without joy—that he had trained well on Huns.

'Tizzy's already started back, with Willy,' Dick said.

'Well, you come all the same. You can ride back on Wood-pigeon afterwards.'

Dick used Woodpigeon to travel backwards and forwards between Flambards and the farm, or to go to the village. Christina loved to watch Dick ride, not for any personal reasons, but for the purely aesthetic satisfaction it gave her to see somebody ride so well. Nobody she knew could handle a horse as Dick could. When there was time she wanted him to try Pheasant.

'Very well, m'—' Dick stopped himself, and smiled.

Christina grinned. She waited while Dick washed and fetched his jacket, and Woodpigeon, whom he hitched behind the cart. The exchange of smiles had given Christina a small jolt, for no reason that she could exactly analyse. Waiting for him, being very honest with herself, she knew there was nothing about Dick that kept her awake at nights (the first symptoms of her love for Will), but, equally well, she knew that she had asked him to supper because she wanted him to talk to; she wanted his company. Every night she ate with Mary and Tizzy. She was not lonely in the accepted sense of the word. But for someone to talk to at her own level she was as lacking as a blade of grass in a desert for water.

Dick joined her in the cart, sitting with his elbows on his knees as he usually did, as if he wanted to ease his chest. Glancing at him, with a slight anxiety, Christina thought that he looked very tired, yet better than the day she had met him in Rotherhithe. Against the brown skin of his neck his hair was pale, the colour of barley, as she had always remembered it (only a good deal longer now, like that of all the men in the village, for the barber had been called up).

'You're all right?' she said. 'You're not overdoing it?'

'No. I feel better than when I came. I get a bit tired, that's all.'

The cart bounced over the rutted tracks. On the far side of the covert they met Willy and Tizzy coming out of the ride, and they sat in the back and Pepper took them all up to the house together. Christina, listening to Tizzy's laugh, and the few words of German exchanged between Willy and Dick, was happy, happier than she had been for what seemed a very long time. The evening sun, touching the oak-trees beyond the house, cast long shadows across the drive. Willy went down to meet his truck and Christina went into the kitchen with Dick.

'Where did you learn your German?' she asked him.

'There were German orderlies in the hospital—prisoners of war. One of them—I got quite friendly with. He taught me a bit of German, and I helped him get on with English.'

Mary had the table laid, and set another place as she saw Dick. A rich savoury smell came from the range, and on the sideboard stood a row of freshly baked loaves. Christina took Isobel upstairs to feed her, very content, conscious of the evening sun, mellow and gold, flooding the landing, very peaceful: the feel of people in the house, of things to look forward to, the smell of hay that came in through the open window. And the baby . . .

'You're a picture-book baby, if I say it myself,' Christina said to her, with utter satisfaction. Isobel's cheeks were the same golden brown as Mary's bread, her eyes very large and dark. She smiled very easily, and cried very little. Strange, Christina thought, that she was Will's; the only offspring Will had ever contemplated were mechanical, the fruits of his drawing-board, his darling machines. 'You should have had wings, my Isobel. He would have understood you then.' Save that he never had the chance.

Christina put the baby in her cot, and went downstairs. Tizzy was washing noisily, having put the horses away.

'We saw the Gothas today,' he told Christina when he came to the table. 'Did you see them?'

'No!' Christina looked anxiously at Dick. 'Did they come over? I heard the gunfire, but it sounded a long way away.'

'Yes, it was. They weren't very close. Over the Thames, I should imagine,' Dick said.

'I saw them,' Tizzy said stubbornly.

'You saw crows, and perhaps a British fighter,' Dick said.

'Gothas,' Tizzy growled, scowling into his pie.

'We'll have to try shooting them, instead of rabbits,' Dick suggested.

'And have Gotha pie!' Tizzy's face lit up. 'Can you shoot an aeroplane down with a rifle?'

'Yes, if you're lucky.' Dick looked warily at Christina, but she said, matter-of-factly, 'Below six thousand feet an aeroplane can be hit by rifle-fire.'

'Can I have a gun?' Tizzy asked.

'No, you cannot!'

When the meal was finished they drank cups of tea, and Christina took the yawning Tizzy up to bed.

'Why can' Uncle Dick live here?' Tizzy asked. 'That ol' farm's dirty.'

'It isn't! I scrubbed it out myself.'

'I wouldn' like to live in it.'

'Oh, you—'

'Uncle Dick could sleep in the room with the aeroplanes in. He could lie in bed and shoo' them down with his gun.'

'Oh, don't talk rubbish.' Christina, disturbed, was short. 'I've told you not to touch those aeroplanes. I hope you haven't been in there, meddling?'

'Jus' looking.'

Christina looked into Will's room on her way downstairs, and saw the model machines still hanging from their cottons over the bed. Made by Will when he was small, they were very quaint now, with the old-fashioned elevators stretched out in front like the antennae of antediluvian insects. They were covered in dust. 'It doesn't matter,' Christina said to herself, determined not to be feeble. 'It's not a museum. Tizzy could play with them if he wanted.' But she knew she wouldn't let him. She went downstairs, carefully not thinking about anything at all.

In the kitchen Mary had cleared away and lit the lamps and was now cutting Dick's hair.

'You men are like a lot of sheep round here these days,' she grumbled. 'I can't stand the sight of you.'

Christina smiled to herself. She sat on a wooden chair in front of the range, and propped her elbows on her knees and stared into the fire, listening to the click of the scissors and the hiss of the lamps. The domesticity of the moment charmed her: she could enjoy it merely for what it was, and not for any significance it might or might not have. 'I can't complain,' she thought, 'not any more. Not with all this. Even if—' And she would not think about the gap, the abyss, the cold bleak pit, watching the fire and Tizzy's dusty boots lying where he had thrown them.

'You'd get a job with the Army any day,' Dick was telling Mary. 'Even they don't crop it any closer.' He stood up, running his hand over the bristles that had been his hair.

Christina laughed. 'You look like a Prussian.'

Dick clicked his heels, Hun style, and barked something in German. Mary sniffed dourly, sweeping up the hair. 'You look like a man, at least.'

'Yes. Thank you very much, Mary. It's a lot better.' He said to Christina, 'I'll go back now. It's getting on.'

'Very well.'

When he had gone Christina went up to bed. She stood at the window, brushing her hair, and in the deep blue dusk she saw Woodpigeon go up the newly cut hay-field towards the covert. He was cantering, a white ghost in the evening, like the white barn-owl flying. Christina watched until he disappeared into the trees.

Christina was frightened. She reined Pheasant into the shade of a big elm-tree in the hedgerow, and stroked his shoulder, but she knew he could feel her fear. The gunfire burst across the

89

sky, looking very pretty—if one felt able to appreciate it. But the thumps of it in her very own fields turned Christina's stomach. The ground shivered, and the sky was full of this unnatural noise. The Gothas were there this time for all the world to see, not only the avid Tizzy. And Christina had no idea where he was just at that moment. She cursed, worried for the children, watching the hideous, clumsy bombers against the bright sky. This was the first time they had come so close, and there had been no warning, only the thumping of the guns.

They were flying in formation, harried by two or three British fighters. Christina, watching, tried not to feel anything but righteous anger and fear, but she was aware of a third dimension, which made the sweat come up on the palms of her hands, feeling the gunfire as it rocked the bombers' wings, the explosions in her own ear-drums, as if it were herself up in the sky. 'It's horrible,' she thought. And above it, the chatter of machine-gun fire from the fighters, and the whining of their sharp, diving attacks, shrill above the heavy German engines. A white sweat broke out on Pheasant's neck, which the reins carved off as he flung up his head. Christina could feel him trembling.

'It's all right, my beauty . . .' Christina hoped very much that it was. If only she had been with the others!

Two of the fighters had chivvied one bomber out of formation and, as she watched, Christina saw the machine stagger. One wing dropped, and it started to fall in a sideslip, a small eddy of white smoke trailing it. Christina felt very sick. She looked away, at Pheasant's gleaming coat with its strange rocking-horse dapples. She found she was praying very hard: 'Please, God, don't let anything happen!' But she could hear the noise of the bomber, a shrill, falling, exhausted crescendo, punctuated by machine-gun fire. It was coming down, but under control now, the thin smoke spiralling behind. It was as if it knew she was there, watching, because it started to make a big circle to miss the covert; Christina knew that it was going to land in her hay-field, if it were lucky, if it kept ahead of the smoke. She stiffened in the saddle, hands clenched in anguish.

'Don't let this happen to me! Please, God, don't let it happen here!'

But she knew that it was going to, and she could not keep her eyes away now, hypnotized by the labouring machine as it cleared the edge of the covert only fifty feet above the highest trees. It was a vast machine, its wings almost eighty feet across, uglier in its extremity than anything Christina had ever seen, trailing torn fabric and mashed spars and the insidious smoke. She saw the letters on its side and its big German crosses, the pilot's face peering, the sun flashing on his goggles. She felt Pheasant's terror, like a current, but he did not move; she heard the whine, like a summer insect, of a fighter far above her, and smelt the sickening, burning smell of oil as it sprayed the field. The machine passed right over her head, blotting out the sun. It weaved in its death flight and went into the ground out of control. Christina watched, rigid, unable even to shut her eyes, and saw the great belly tear into dry earth, scattering clods and bits of metal in all directions. A stench of dust and burning fuel went up in a cloud and into it the splitting and groaning and cracking of every broken part as it came to its violent rest splayed and spattered and spewed all over the July grass. When it was still and silent, Christina heard herself moaning. It was quite unreal, as disasters had always been to Christina in the first instant; her brain could not accept, even with the evidence, until the minutes had gone by, and nothing had proved otherwise.

But an instinct moved her, completely without her wanting to do anything, and she found she was urging Pheasant out of the shelter of the elm and galloping towards the wreckage. When Pheasant's courage failed him, and he wheeled away, half-rearing, she slid off him and ran, sobbing and cursing, spurred by a rage and a pity that was near hysteria. Even the smell of smoke did not stop her.

The pilot was struggling to free himself from an entanglement of crumpled metal. He shouted something to Christina and pointed behind him to the rear-gunner's cockpit. Christina, suddenly very sane, climbed up over the wreckage of the wings and came to the cockpit just as the pilot freed himself and scrambled clear. Christina looked, and saw a dangling arm, a boy's face as white as a daisy petal, and more blood than she knew the human body possessed. She just stood, as if it were her own blood drained, and looked. She thought, strangely, 'Why, he's got a haircut like Dick's!' And then, her petrified brain moving out of its shock, she turned away and saw the whole

hay-field start to turn upside down before her very eyes. Someone shouted at her. She heard the voice, sharp and furious,
'Christina!' and a hand on her arm, dragging her brutally away
out of the wreckage. 'Get away, you fool!'

Across the hay-field people were running in a ragged stream.
She saw them, far away, coming from the village. And close to,
Dick's face, very intense, turning away. She heard the German
shouting, and Dick left her and went back into the wreckage
with the pilot. 'But he's dead!' she screamed after him. 'It's no
good! He's dead!' The smoke was thickening out of the twisted
wreckage, and darkening in colour, hanging against the blue
sky. She saw the first bright thread of flame. She knew all about
aeroplanes; she knew what would happen. And she remembered
that Gothas had a crew of three, and there was another man in
it. She started to cry, standing there, not going forward or back.
The pilot was tearing at something in the smoke, and Dick was
holding something, bending over. She heard the sharp exchange
of words, the urgency, and saw Dick kicking holes in the wreckage and rending away splintered wood, pulling at something.
The smoke billowed on the summer breeze and covered them
up.

The people coming from the village stayed away in a big
semicircle. Only the little grey figure of Wilhelm came running,
his face contorted with fear. Christina, seeing him, started back
for the machine, remembered Tizzy and the baby, and stopped,
wavering. The flames were taking hold, but now the huddle of
figures emerged, dragging, half carrying the third man, stumbling over the grass. Although they were hurrying, they seemed
to Christina infinitely slow, weighed down by the inert bundle.
Christina started to back away, watching, converging to meet
them, and two bolder men came out of the bunch of spectators,
and reached out for the stupid trailing limbs, so that the pace
quickened: the little knot of men was running, and the flames
started to leap up behind them, running out in small tongues
across the gleanings of hay. Christina turned round then and
ran, too, and some of the villagers, not knowing what was going
on, started to move away, still staring—for all the world,
Christina thought, like a herd of bullocks. But some of them
went up to Dick and the Germans, and the injured man was laid
in the grass, and Christina joined them.

Dick said something to her. She didn't know what, the words were drowned in the explosion from the burning Gotha. A hot blast swept the field and bits of wood and metal spat past in all directions. Christina ducked instinctively, covering her face with her hands. She did not take them away in any hurry, because she felt she had seen enough. She wanted to go away. She heard some women crying, and the little boys shouting with excitement, running for souvenirs, and all she wanted now was Pheasant, and the quietness of the covert, and to ride home, not seeing any more.

'Christina.'

Dick was beside her. 'You shouldn't have gone,' he said. 'Not for a German.'

'They're all the same,' she said, remembering the boy's face. Dick had gone, but she did not say so. She didn't want to say anything.

'I'll come home with you,' he said. 'You shouldn't have looked. You shouldn't have gone.'

The local policeman had taken charge behind them, and the whole village was there to help him. They walked to the edge of the covert, where Pheasant was grazing, and Dick went to

catch him, while Christina waited. The excitement was a field's length away now, quite insignificant, the smoke dying, the people picking round, little black crows. A rabbit ran out of the covert. Between Christina and the dead boy's funeral pyre there was an expanse of summer grass, her own grass, with skylarks nesting in it. But even the skylarks, she thought, had the reaper, and the rabbits had Dick's gun. There was no point in getting sentimental.

Dick came back with Pheasant.

'I don't want to ride,' Christina said. 'Just walk. You can never just *sit* on Pheasant, and I don't feel like coping.'

Dick led Pheasant and they walked back in silence. Christina could feel tears falling down her cheeks, and yet she was not aware of crying. The woods were cool and quiet, with only the rattle of pigeons flying away and their soft throaty calls. But the village people were like vultures picking, Christina thought.

Dick put Pheasant in a loose-box and unsaddled him.

'Come up to the house,' Christina said. 'Mary will get you a drink. You don't look too good.' The smoke had affected him, and he was coughing, and walked hunched, as if his chest was hurting him. Christina was glad he didn't talk or fuss; she knew that she would not be able to stomach Mary's fuss. She left Dick in the kitchen to cope with the excitement, and went into her own sitting-room and locked the door.

Everything she thought she had put behind her, that she thought time had softened, came back as if not even one day had passed since she had had the telegram from France. She knew now what it was like in fact, not merely in her imagination. She went to the bureau and got out the little bundle of letters which she still remembered word for word, although she had not looked at them for months. She was past being cool now, and rational; she was going to give in, she was defeated. 'Today,' she thought, 'just today, I can't help myself.'

Besides Will's letters there were the bits and pieces, the citation out of the newspaper for his D.S.O., the little oily scrap of paper with 'I love you' written on it which he had given her when they had flown the Channel (and nearly fallen in it), the awful telegram, the description of their wedding which Dorothy had kept for them, out of the local newspaper, and the letter from Will's C.O., the letters from his friends, and the letter from

Sergeant Andrews, whom she had never met. She smoothed out this blotched and painfully composed message and read it.

'I am writing to you because the C.O. said to write to you, to say what happened. First I am very sorry what happened also that Captain Russell saved my life—' (Having pondered on this before, Christina had come to the conclusion that Sergeant Andrews's grammar was at fault, rather than that he was sorry that Will had saved his life. She thought he meant exactly the opposite.) 'No one except him could got the plane down in one piece even if not wounded but he did and mortally wounded so you understand what I think about him also everyone here.

'We went to take photos of a bombing raid on Wervicq we took photos at 6000 feet the bombs dropped all round us and the archie (guns) was very bad but Mr. Russell did not take evading action because of getting the pictures. We got the pictures but an archie got us it broke a wing spar and knocked up the tail boom so the tail was only on by a bracing wire it was very tender I thought Mr. Russell would have to land but he made for the lines I thought the machine would break up any minute. He got down in a field the right side of the lines I got out and I saw then Mr. Russell was very bad I did not know. A shell splinter gone right through him I knew it was no good. Some Tommies come up and got him out and a M.O. he said it was no good he went to fetch something but Mr. Russell died before he come back. He did not say anything or leave a message I am sorry I know you would ask but he did not. I am sorry to write you this and hope you will get over it as quick as can be expected everyone is sorry there was nobody better than Mr. Russell and you can see any other pilot I would be in in the same place now.'

So now Christina saw it all very clearly, right to the breeze in the grass, and the people converging, the smell of scorched fabric. And why he had not left her a message, although he had been conscious, for she could see now that in such a bloody extremity one did not easily compose a dying message. And if she felt so bitter now, why had she been so thrilled when Will was alive, singing his brave songs about the 'poor aviator'? She had been proud of him, fighting for his country—it was the

96

thing to do; she had been as stupid as all the girls, thinking it was so marvellous. And when it was ended so disgustingly, with all that blood, and he had been given another medal, for dying, what was there left to think then? Did one censor the mind, adoring the courage, ignoring the ignominy of the physical fact of dying, of jerking out the last searing lungfuls of breath beneath the hardened gaze of a handful of Tommies who would shortly—as in the song—'carry the fragments away'? Where was courage then, in exchanging life for a few photographs of destruction for the Army files? It was mere foolishness, the same as Dick bothering to get the German. When you were dead, what then?

Christina sat on the floor, with all the letters scattered around her, and wept, as much from anger as from anything else. She wanted these things to make sense, and they didn't. Most of all she wanted Will to come back, and he wouldn't. She wanted, *wanted* Will . . . wanted the fading image to come into focus so that she could see him again clearly, sprawled in the Surrey heather with the sun in his eyes, laughing, teasing her, trying to teach her the aerodynamics of a bee ('Oh, you fool,' she had said, 'as if it matters!')—even to see him preoccupied, not thinking about her at all, his face tight, almost scowling, as he considered some problem of design. But it was blurred: the phrase 'passed away' seemed suddenly to have a specific meaning. In its hackneyed syllables it held the irrevocability of this gradual fading in a way that Christina only now appreciated.

She read his letters all over again. 'I am wallowing in it,' she thought, and then she didn't even care about that. She lay on the floor and cried without restraint, until she was too exhausted to cry any more.

Chapter 9

Tizzy's souvenir from the Gotha, a large fragment of propeller blade, was his most treasured possession. He propped it up on the mantelshelf in his bedroom, beside Mark's point-to-point trophy, and admired it every night. Christina, forced to admire it, too, found the exercise good for her sensibilities, dulling the raw nerves by sheer boredom, eventually.

'You and your old Gotha!'

Tizzy leapt up and down on the bed, arms outstretched, making whining, bomb-dropping noises. Christina sat patiently, dreaming. It was impossible to get cross with Tizzy; if only he had known it, she could deny him nothing. Even Pheasant was going to get schooled by Dick—when he had time—so that Tizzy could ride him. Christina's excuse was that Pheasant should be more than a one-woman horse—'What if I had to sell him?'—but her argument would not convince Dick. He teased her gently: 'It's so that Fowler can ride him? Or we can use him on the farm? So that Harry can go down to the village on him when there's a message to be taken?'

'Of course,' Christina replied, very solemn.

But just now there wasn't time. The barley was silver, waist high, and Dick said the South Field was ready to cut. So it had started, this harvest that Christina had thought would never happen. 'It's the miracle of the century,' she told Dick, and Dick now referred to the operation as the Miracle of the Century. Christina, watching the first circle of the binder, felt that she was surfacing again, after the Gotha. The corn had grown, and Isobel was sitting up in the baby-carriage, laughing. 'What more do you want?' Christina asked herself.

Tizzy, the Gotha, nearly went through the springs.

'Tizzy, stop it! I thought you were tired!'

He had been out in the fields all day, staggering with barley traves in his arms as big as himself. His thin, agile body was all weals and pricks from the barbs. How like Mark he was! Christina, catching a certain expression on his face as he at last collapsed between the sheets, was pierced again by his uncanny reawakening in her mind, so that Mark was quite close, alive, grinning in his old careless way. 'He is like Mark in his ways,' she thought. Not only the looks. It was not a thought that made her particularly glad. Mark had been arrogant and brutal, as well as gay and bold and extremely handsome. The last time she had seen him, before he went to France, she thought he had mellowed a little, perhaps become a little more sympathetic, and he had told her himself that he had 'grown up'. But as she looked at Tizzy she remembered Mark lying in the very same bed barely conscious the night Dick had beaten him up. She had had to sit with him nearly all night, on the same chair she was sitting on now, and she remembered that most of that night, holding Mark's hand, she had thought about Dick: Dick appearing out of the gloom of that winter evening, months after he had been dismissed from Flambards, to inflict that awful damage on Mark, Dick who—until that moment—had always been to Christina the embodiment of kindness. And the reason for Dick's onslaught had been—and how could you not laugh, Christina thought, the way things turned out?—the same child she was now kissing good night. Dick had beaten up Mark for getting Violet 'into trouble'. And the trouble had been Tizzy. And now Tizzy was Dick's favourite human being. Life's surprises never stopped.

Christina drew the curtains against the summer dusk. How complicated it was going to be, she thought, when Tizzy asked who his father was. And, even, who she was. He called her 'Ma' now, in a friendly, casual way, and Christina accepted it quite happily, although Mary said it was vulgar and he wanted a clip round the ear. He called Isobel his sister, Dick his uncle (which was true) and Mary 'that old woman'. And Fowler was the only suggestion he had come up with for her own husband. Dick, Tizzy said, should live with them at Flambards. Tizzy did not understand the ramifications involved, the tangle of law, tradition, and emotion that the prospect invoked. But Christina, listening to the blackbirds in the chestnut-trees, did not think Tizzy's idea out of place. She realized how very much she had come to depend upon Dick. But she did not want to think further about this now. She was not ready.

She went downstairs. Since the builders had been in, the wide hall with its tiled floor repaired, and ornate doorways painted, and the plaster renewed and whitewashed, looked almost gracious (which she had always believed was possible). She had polished the chairs and the oak chest and the mahogany table herself, and put a bowl of the tangled garden roses on the table. Their scent was heavy in the dusk, their pink faces opened out showing stamens bowed with thick pollen, shedding petals and gold-dust—untidy, blowsy perfection. Christina remembered her dreams; she remembered the children's voices and the groom waiting at the door with the ponies. She had it all. 'Only the groom is in the kitchen,' she thought, 'waiting to dine with the mistress of the house.' That had not been in her dreams; it did not conform to the *Ladies' Journal* influence that had inspired her picture in the first place. In the *Ladies' Journal* the working man kept his place and the lady hers. Christina frowned.

There was a letter on the table. Christina scooped it up. It was from Aunt Grace. 'I hope to come and see you and stay a few days very shortly. I cannot wait to see the dear baby . . .' Aunt Grace had been ill when Isobel was born, and had been convalescing all during the summer months at Broadstairs. Christina's frown deepened: she had yet to tell Aunt Grace about Tizzy. She knew Aunt Grace would be horrified, and had reasoned that the state of the woman's health was a good reason for delaying the shock. And what would Aunt Grace think of the groom in the kitchen? Christina's mouth tightened ominously. Seeing her ménage as she knew that Aunt Grace was going to see it, she was not surprised that the mahogany table had received no calling-cards, to go with the bowl of roses.

Dick was sitting at the table with a tankard of beer. He had been driving the binder all day and was covered with a fur of dust, fine as the rose pollen. He no longer stood up when Christina came into the room.

'Aunt Grace is coming to stay,' she said with a grimace.

Mary, fetching a leg of boiled ham and a big dish of potatoes to the table, said, 'God save us! What shall we say about Tizzy?'

'She'll have to know some time. She's very kind really. Only old-fashioned,' Christina said.

'I'd best keep down at the farm,' Dick said.

Christina said, 'We've nothing to hide.'

Dick looked at her, not smiling at all. 'No,' he said. And Christina knew that there was a good deal of meaning in the one word, and she felt a slight stir of misgiving, and a pleasure beneath it that surprised her. To cover it she said, 'I hope she waits till we've completed the Miracle of the Century.'

Dick smiled then, and said, 'She won't, I dare say.'

They all worked now, even Mary in the afternoons, and some women from the village, while the weather held fair. Aunt Grace would get little attention if she came now.

'Well, she was born here. She understands the harvest won't wait.' Christina picked a barley barb out of the sleeve of her dress while Mary carved the bacon. She knew now that she would miss Dick at supper if he didn't come. She had come to take his presence for granted, his unassuming way, taking no liberties, yet without deference, merely honest—as he had always been. He had had no formal education, but his native intelligence was greater than her own. And Christina remembered, from long ago, Will saying that it was luck, what you were born into, and Dick's bad luck that he had been born without advantage, his own good luck that he had been born with. Only Will had divided it into 'slaves and slave-drivers'. But the war, Christina thought, made no such distinction, killing them in equal proportion. The war, she thought, by neglect of respecting one's station in life, had made such arguments superfluous. Will had seen it then, before the war made it plain.

A week later, when Christina was just about to take the beer down to the fields for the break, a village boy came to the front door with a telegram. It said, 'Send transport to meet the two-thirty from Liverpool Street.' There was no signature, although she inquired of the boy. And it was addressed merely to Flambards. 'Oh, bother Aunt Grace,' Christina thought. And then, remembering that Aunt Grace had harboured her kindly when she had run away from home, she was ashamed, and gave the boy twopence. 'She can take Isobel for walks. She'll love that,' she thought. 'She can ride Woodpigeon.' This made her laugh out loud.

Fowler was of more use to Dick in the fields than she was herself, so Christina harnessed Pepper to the trap and drove down to the station on her own. 'She's bound to love Tizzy when she meets him,' she thought. Or was she? Tizzy was not invariably lovable, not when his underlip went out and his eyebrows came down like his father's.

It was warm and Pepper was in no hurry. Christina saw the train huffing away across the field before she came into the station approach. An unhitched van of heifers was bellowing in the siding and a small trickle of afternoon shoppers straggled away with their bags and bundles. Christina could not see Aunt Grace, although she could picture her waiting, her luggage beside her, pursing her lips. Christina pushed back her untidy hair, and pulled Pepper to a halt outside the station entrance. There was nobody there, save a soldier talking to the station-master. He turned round as Christina went through the doorway.

'Hullo, Christina,' he said.

It was Mark.

The shock to Christina was so great that her mind blanked out. She would have fallen if the station-master hadn't had the presence of mind to leap forward and divert her on to the station bench. She saw the oil lamps and the prices of the return tickets to London making parabolas round her head, and Mark laughing. She heard the blood singing in her ears. Mark came

towards her and she stood up and put her arms round him, burying her face against all the sharp little insignias that decorated his uniform. He had to hold her, or she would have fallen. She could not think . . . She felt his hand stroke her hair, felt the roughness of his chin on her forehead, and heard him laughing.

'Here—' He scooped in his pocket and tossed a coin to the station-master. 'Fetch her some brandy from the Arms.'

'They're shut, sir. It's the new law. But there's some in the first-aid box in the office.'

'I'm all right,' Christina said faintly.

They sat her on the bench and made her drink the brandy. She watched Mark, unable to take her eyes away, her face bluish-white, cold as ice. Her mind was quite numb. She took in his amused face, the dark eyes with the hint of scorn, his easy, lithe figure, thinner than it had been, impatient as always.

'Don't look so pleased!' he was saying, teasing. 'It's not at all complimentary!'

'Mark, I—oh! I can't—'

'Come on,' he said. 'Let's get home.'

He pulled her to her feet, and they went outside. The sunshine hit Christina like gunfire. The station-master loaded the luggage and Mark helped Christina up into the cart. Then he got up beside her and took the reins.

He said, 'I've waited a long time to see all this again! How is the old place? Any horses to ride?'

Christina looked at him again. She could not believe it. And the brandy warmed her blood, and her mind lurched.

'Mark!' She put her elbow on her knees and leaned her head in her hands. 'Mark, it's eighteen months since—'

'Oh, you knew I'd turn up, surely? They sent you "Missing", I suppose? They were damned right—"Missing" covers a whole lot of nasty eventualities, believe me!'

'But why didn't you write?'

'You can't write from a Turkish prison.'

'But—' Oh, she would learn later—but how typical of Mark! Christina's emotions, struggling to life, were the same mixture that Mark had always aroused in her, with indignation taking an upper hand. And she was appalled. The joy she should feel at seeing him was eclipsed with petty rage at his thoughtlessness, and with a further horror that she should not feel unabated joy.

'Does Aunt Grace know?'

'I called on her when I got into London, but they said she was in Broadstairs. I went down there and saw her, and then came on here.'

Christina pictured Aunt Grace, in her convalescent state, keeling into insensibility on her boarding-house doorstep.

'Oh, Mark, you should—oh, I don't know! It's like seeing a ghost—'

'I asked around a bit, to find out what was going on. Some-one at your old address said you were down here—I called at that place in Kingston. Thought I might see Dorothy, but no luck. And they told me Will had copped it, which was no great surprise, seeing what he did for a living.' He leaned forward and gave the amiable Pepper a clout with the doubled ends of the reins. Pepper snorted with surprise and plunged into a rapid trot from his normal steady jog. 'These the only sort of nags you can get at home these days?'

Christina was silent. His casual mention of Will had speared her, made her feel physically sick. If it had been Will— She wanted to cry out. Yet she loved Mark with the loyalty of family; he was her brother, in a sense.

'Tell me what's been happening,' he said. 'What's going on at Flambards? Old Fowler still there? The place still falling down?'

Christina almost swooned at the prospect that loomed ahead. Three miles farther on, to be precise. How to say to Mark about the people that now inhabited Flambards, including his own son? And Dick . . . Christina licked her lips.

'You'll see some changes.' She was hardly able to make words pass her lips.

She watched him, scarcely aware of what was happening, only of his figure beside her, cap pushed back, lips clicking to Pepper. There was still the broken tooth that Dick had knocked out, and the scar through his eyebrow, the Romanesque emphasis on the broken nose. God in heaven— And she had gone to meet Aunt Grace! Old Mary and Fowler would die of shock.

'Mark, I must warn Mary, at least. It might kill her, if you walk in—and Fowler. They're old now, you know—'

'They'll love it!' he laughed. 'But if you like, if you think so—'

And Dick, Christina thought. Her heart gave a wild, in-voluntary swing. And Tizzy . . . 'Meet your father.'

'Mark, I ought to tell you—'

'I'd give anything to have Treasure back with me. I last saw him at Gallipoli. And that chestnut, Goldwillow. He was a goer. What is there to ride?'

'Only Woodpigeon.' And Pheasant. Christina did not want Mark to ride Pheasant. 'And a bay—too small for you. I ride him.'

'I wish cubbing had started!'

'There's no pack now. It was split up. There's been no hunting the last three winters.'

'Oh, God, and I always thought that was what I was fighting for! I can tell you, I thought about this old place a good deal when I was out there—it's the only thing that kept me going at times. Most of the chaps thought about women, but if I wanted to cheer myself up I thought of hounds running. They used to think I was a bit touched.'

Christina could not say anything. At Pepper's enlivened pace they were now already half-way to Flambards, where the oblivious harvest would be progressing; Mary would be on her way back from the fields with Isobel, Tizzy setting up his traves, Dick watching his machine, keeping the horses in just the right place. Dick . . . Christina clenched her hands, a sense of panic rising up in her. The thought that Dick might go away made her feel physically ill. She shut her eyes, feeling the shock again, Mark's elbow against hers. She was listening to Mark, and seeing Dick on the binder, Dick in the kitchen drinking beer. Dick had become a rock in her life. The sense of shock almost overcame her. In five minutes they were up to the Flambards gates.

'It's just the same as ever,' Mark was saying, with enormous satisfaction.

Christina was unable to contradict.

'I do believe you've tidied the old place up! I've never seen the park so neat for years. Whose money did you use?'

'My own. If you left any for the purpose, you certainly took pains not to tell anybody where you kept it.' The sharpness was instinctive, the old sharpness that Mark had always pricked off in her. She was amazed to hear herself talk so bitterly—and Mark out of his grave for scarcely half an hour. But he laughed. And Christina was ashamed. Her feelings were so shredded, she was unable to make sense of anything.

She said, 'You'd better drive round to the stables. There's no one to take Pepper.'

'Where's Fowler, then?'

'He's in the fields, helping with the harvest.'

'Whose fields?'

'On the farm. Your farm.' Christina's voice shook. She

thought: '*Your* farm, *your* son, *your* house, *your* employees,' and she was so ashamed of her feelings she could not make her voice say anything else.

Mark was surprised. 'It takes a war, then, to make a farm pay. Whose doing was this, then? Yours? Who is farming it?'

'I started it off. The men do the work now.'

They got down from the trap. This was her opportunity to mention Dick. Mark was looking at her, not bothered with the horse, who moved off to help himself to a drink.

'You're a goer, Christina, aren't you? You always were.'

Christina could not mention Dick. It was impossible.

'I never could understand why you married Will when you could have married me and had all this.'

'I didn't love you. Is that such a detail?'

'Is that why you don't look particularly pleased to see me again?'

'Mark—please!'

'Aunt Grace told me you had a child. That surprised me.'

'Yes.' It had surprised her, too, she remembered.

'Pity it was only a girl.'

'I don't mind. I'm only a girl, too.'

Mark laughed, not unkindly. 'Come on, Christina, let's not fight already.'

'Oh, Mark!' She was half laughing, half crying, completely at a loss. 'I can't take it in! I—'

'Cheer up. I wanted to make you happy, coming home.'

'Yes—oh, I'm sorry! I am. I just feel—oh, dizzy. Stupid. I can't help it.'

'I suppose you'd rather I was Will.'

'Will won't come home. They buried him.'

'Oh, I'm sorry, Christina. My turn now. We seem to be saying all the wrong things. Let's put this nag away and go up to the house. What a ruddy ghost of a stable! This is the first time I've seen it empty.'

'Yes. I hated it when I came home. It seemed the worst thing of all.'

They put Pepper in his box, stripping his harness and hanging it on its pegs, amicable suddenly. Mark had always said outrageous things; he was utterly insensitive, but he was not given to brooding and rancour; he was usually laughing

107

half an hour after the most bitter quarrel. They walked back to the house, arm in arm, suddenly in accord. Christina, still white, found she was laughing. She had wanted people, she remembered. And had the people that belonged to Flambards ever lived amicably together, like a normal family? No. From the very first moment she had entered the place she had been conscious of the discord. So why should it be any different now, merely after a period of time? They were the same people. They would pick up where they left off. She had forgotten all these basic truths in her own emotional home-coming last year. Wanting the people, she had forgotten how they had all hated each other when they had been alive together in this place.

They went into the kitchen.

Mark threw his cap on the table and unfastened his belt, pulled at his tie. He had grey in his hair, Christina noticed. His hair was exactly like Will's. She sat down aware that her legs were shaking. He was a captain, the same as Will.

'Tell me—' she started.

'Uncle Dick sent me for the beer,' said a familiar voice from the doorway. Tizzy stood there, four-square, the harvest dust powdering his brown face and untidy hair. He looked at Mark, lowering his brows suspiciously.

'Who's that man?' he said to Christina.

Christina looked at Mark. He was grinning at Tizzy, slightly puzzled, but not at all thunderstruck. 'Can't he *see*?' Christina thought. And then, because Mark had surprised her all but into insensibility, she turned to Tizzy and said deliberately, 'He's your father.'

'He's not,' said Tizzy, without much interest. 'Uncle Dick is my father.'

Christina had not up to that point realized just what a tangle Tizzy's mind was in as far as relationships were concerned. But she ignored this fact for the time being and watched Mark take in the significance of her remark. He was watching Tizzy reach up for the beer cans that stood on the dresser. His eyes narrowed and he stopped pulling at his tie and said to Christina, 'What did you say?'

'I said you are his father.'

'Who the hell is his mother, then?'

'Violet.'

108

'Violet!'

Christina's revelation had all the effect she had desired. Mark sat back as if he had been winded, his hand falling down on the table. He watched Tizzy, who carried on filling the beer cans out of the barrel. Christina saw the amazement, the disbelief, change slowly into genuine interest. He sat up again, never taking his eyes off Tizzy.

'What's he doing here, then?' he asked softly.

'I've adopted him.'

'Come here,' Mark said to Tizzy.

Tizzy looked at Mark dubiously. 'Have you killed a lot of Huns?'

'Yes,' Mark said. He laughed. 'Why, is that what you'd like to do?'

'Oh, yes! Only not Wilhelm. We got a Gotha come down, an' one of them was killed, wasn't he, Ma? It come down in the hay-field and set on fire, an' I got a piece of it in my bedroom. I'm going to be a soldier.'

'Good for you.'

'I got to take the beer.'

'Yes. Very important.'

Christina said to him, 'Tell Fowler that Mark's come home.' She wanted to say, 'Tell Dick.' She wanted to endow Tizzy with the power to convey her feelings to Dick, but it was impossible. He would learn what had happened, and his feelings were his own affair, no concern of hers. (Only she was concerned.)

Tizzy picked up the beer cans. 'How many Huns you killed?' he asked Mark.

'Oh, dozens. And scores of Turks.'

Tizzy hesitated. 'I must take the beer,' he said regretfully, and retreated out of the kitchen.

Mark watched him go, grinning. 'Well,' he said to Christina, 'I thought of all sorts of things that might have happened while I was away, but he wasn't one of them. A ready-made son.'

He did not inquire after Violet. He sat looking very pleased with himself, slightly bemused. 'He must have been born the year Treasure ran second to Allington's Mayflower. That would be nineteen eleven. So he's—what?—six. Well, there's not many fathers I know of who get delivered of a six-year-old son.

Any more surprises, Christina? Let's have them all while we're about it.'

Christina steeled herself. 'There's Dick,' she said. 'He works here. He runs the farm.'

Mark's expression changed abruptly. He looked at Christina sharply. 'So! That's how it is!'

Christina, very controlled, said, 'I employ him. He lives in the farm-house. He comes here for his supper some nights, that's all.'

'How did he manage to get out of the Army?'

'He was wounded, and got T.B.'

'So he came whining back here for a job?'

Christina's eyes took on a different expression. 'Did Dick ever whine? In spite of all that happened to him? Be fair, Mark. Be careful what you say.'

'All right. Let's put it that he knew Will and I were safely out of the way—'

'He knew nothing until I went to Rotherhithe to ask him to come and work here. And then he refused.'

'Oh, I can believe that! And you pleading with him!'

'He said he wasn't fit enough to take a job. He came six months later, and since then the farm has never looked back. You can ask Fowler or Mary, or any of them, what the truth is, and they will tell you.'

'He was always sweet on you, right from the start. I bet I know what his game is!'

'Oh, Mark, grow up! A lot has happened since we were children together. Haven't you noticed?'

'What was I supposed to notice locked up in a Turkish prison camp? How was I supposed to know what was going on? If I can come back here and find I have a son six years old—'

'Mark, you knew you had a child before the war ever started. Don't tell me *you* didn't know why Violet was dismissed!'

His abrupt reversal from attack to self-pity made Christina despair. She had never been able to have a coherent argument with Mark because of his wild, illogical switches of reasoning; they had bickered all through their childhood, through most of their subsequent meetings, and now they were at it again within an hour of Mark's miraculous resurrection. And always Christina had been infuriated by this inconsequence of Mark's, his childlike switches away from the point of the disagreement.

'You're impossible to argue with! You distort everything out of focus. You always have done.'

'Oh, well, let's not argue,' he said, switching again. 'Get me some of that beer and something to eat. I don't want to spoil everything by thinking of that swine Dick. Just let him keep out of my way, that's all.'

Christina, with the biggest effort of self-control she had ever made in her life, fetched Mark a glass of beer.

Chapter 10

'I don't think there is room at Flambards for both of us—
Captain Russell and me,' Dick said. 'I'll see the harvest through,
and then I'll get another job.'

He was harnessing up the horses in the farm stable, ready for
another day's work. Stanley and Harry were in the yard ready
to take the wagons out to the fields, surprised by Christina's
early appearance. Christina, after a sleepless night torn by the
most painful confusions, leaned against the partition watching
Dick. She was trying to guess how he must have taken the news,
carelessly announced by Tizzy out in the field. She realized
that she had been thinking of him most of the time since then,
all during the evening when people had kept calling from the
village—the Vicar, Dr. Porter, Mr. Masters, and several of

the old hunting people—when Fowler had been drunk in the kitchen and Mary had been weeping over the festive supper, when she had gone to bed and heard Mark stumbling uncertainly up the stairs, falling over Marigold and swearing. She had thought of Dick eating his supper in his own kitchen, and Dick lying on his bed, staring at the moonlight on the walls, marked into patterns by the lacework of pear twigs across the windows.

'Don't go away,' she said.

'I don't want to go away. But you know as well as I do that Mr. Mark and I don't mix.'

'He's still in the Army. He's only home on leave.' Christina's voice quivered with disgust at her own disloyalty. Was she suggesting that when he had gone back to the front, possibly to get killed properly the next time, everything at Flambards would be back to normal? She knew that it could never be the same again.

'I will work for you, but not for him,' Dick said. 'If he is the owner of Flambards now—well, you can see that, Christina.'

He had never called her Christina before, except during the crisis beside the crashed Gotha. Christina leaned her head back against the partition, against the cushion of her hastily pinned-up hair.

'It will work out,' she said, with a conviction she did not feel. 'Please wait before you decide anything. Please don't go away.'

Dick looked at her over the horse's back, not saying anything. Christina, aware that she was not acting the part of an employer, straightened up angrily. What she really wanted to tell Dick was that she did not, nor ever would, love Mark enough to marry him, even for the sake of possessing Flambards, but this was not a thing an employer said to an employee.

'Does he know who Tizzy is?' Dick asked.

Christina nodded. Dick's face seemed to tighten in a curious, blank way. He pulled the horse's tail through the crupper and bent to do up the girths. 'Will you tell Wilhelm to come straight down to the bottom field? The boys are taking the wagons.'

'Yes.'

There was nothing else to say. Christina went back to Flambards and breakfasted with Mark. He looked more familiar in a white shirt and dirty old breeches, and was in a very amiable mood, regaling Tizzy with extremely tall stories about Army life. Christina could see that the two of them had taken to each other in a big way. Tizzy's directness appealed to Mark, and Mark reacted by speaking to the boy in an easy, man-to-man way, obviously amused by his new role. Tizzy, who usually darted from the table as soon as he had finished his last mouthful, lingered today, hanging on Mark's words. Christina, remembering Dick's expression, said, 'Go along, Tizzy, if you've finished.' She saw immediately that the difficult relationship between the three of them was going to be infinitely complicated by the child.

'What is there for me to ride, then?' Mark asked Christina, turning from Tizzy. 'I'd like to have a look round all the old haunts.'

'There's only Woodpigeon and Pepper. And Woodpigeon's up at the farm—Dick uses him.'

'There's Pheasan',' Tizzy put in. 'Pheasan's the best.'

'Pheasant is too small for Mark. Run along, Tizzy.'

'Is that the bay turned out in the park? That's a nice beast. Where d'you pick him up?'

Christina explained. She felt a fierce possessive spark burn in her. She would not have Mark riding Pheasant.

'Pity he's not a hand higher,' Mark said. 'I'll have to borrow something while I'm here. Masters got anything these days? Or Lucas? What a pretty pass things have come to here!'

'We could ride over to Masters' place and see.'

'Yes, that's an idea. Let's have a lazy day or two, before we bother our heads about business. I'll send off a wire to old Perkins'—Perkins was the family solicitor—'and ask him to come down, but no hurry. I want to know how much money I've got—better not get depressed too early on.' He grinned at Christina, and said, 'I suppose this upsets the apple-cart for you rather? You must have thought the old place was all yours?' Have you seen Perkins about it?'

'Naturally,' Christina said, very cool. 'He applied to the Probate Court six months ago, and got the Letters of Administration.'

'Did he now?' Mark said. 'We'll have to undo his good work again then, won't we?' He paused. 'There's one way you could have it, you know. Even now.'

'How am I supposed to interpret that remark?'

'You know perfectly well. I said all along it was the obvious course of action to take, only you had to go and get infatuated with Will. How much good that did you, I don't know, fastening yourself to the world's only human flying-machine. But you've not missed your chances altogether. I'm still willing.'

'What are you trying to do? Insult me or propose to me?'

'Propose.'

'Why do you think anything has changed?'

'But of course it's changed. Will's out of the way for a start. Be practical, Christina. It's such an obvious solution to everything—my property, your money. We both like the same things—we can carry on just how it always was. The war won't go on for ever. As soon as it's over there'll be hunting again, and we can do the old place up, have lots of children. What's wrong with it for an idea?'

'It would be convenient, I grant you.' Christina's voice was low and angry.

'Well, then? If we don't marry you'll have to clear out, I'll be left with the old place falling to pieces round my ears, and you'll be starting from scratch, looking for a home. I suppose you'd find one all right, but you'd never find a place you'd love like this one. This *is* your home.'

'I don't deny that. I do love this place. But I don't love you.'

'No. Look, I'm not such a fool as you think I am. There's nothing between us like there was between Will and you, I know that. But we know each other, Christina—all the worst bits as well as the better bits. We'd know what to expect.'

Christina's anger fizzled out in an exasperated sigh. Everything Mark said was perfectly true; how could she possibly be angry with such a frank appraisal of the facts, such a lucid, clear-cut proposition? And, certainly, it would be convenient.

'It's impossible, Mark. I wish it wasn't impossible, but it is.' She wasn't brutal enough to explain the simple fact that Mark wasn't the sort of man she wanted as a husband. His father shone through him, and she remembered his father too well. She was quite clear-headed enough to know that there would never be anything for her again like there had been with Will, but to marry Mark for sheer convenience would be carrying convenience to extremes.

And Mark, infuriating as always, now chose to exhibit the undeniably charming side of his nature by laughing in a perfectly friendly fashion, without any ill feeling at all.

'All right. It'll work itself out, I dare say. Let's not think about it again. Let's go and see Masters, eh? I'll ride the carriage nag and you can show off on that smart bay.'

The smart bay gave her an exhilarating ride to Mickleditch, so that she was in a very good mood when all the Masters household came out to greet Mark, the boys even coming up from the rick-yard to drink to the occasion. Amy did not take her eyes off Mark, reminding Christina that Mark attracted nearly every girl he met. 'Perhaps he'll fall for Amy,' she thought, but the moment's optimism gave way instantly to a positive dislike at the idea of Amy usurping her own place at Flambards. A strong feeling of jealousy reminded her of her new insecurity. Her own future was now completely uncertain; the precious roots she had managed to put down had been ripped out. Even her social situation—judging from a remark Mrs. Masters made to her—was indelicate, the bored gossips of the neighbourhood avid to know the relationship between the officer and his widowed sister-in-law, living together at Flambards.

Masters senior offered Mark the use of his own horse for the length of his leave: a champing, heavyweight chestnut called Hannibal.

'I'm afraid he's not fit, but I think you'll find he's got plenty of go.'

Mark was pleased with the horse, and rode him home with Christina, leading Pepper by his side.

'We'll go back through the home farm,' he decided. 'I want to see all this corn you've managed to grow.'

'So this is it,' Christina thought. The confrontation of Mark and Dick . . . She felt her pulse quicken, agreeing by a nod of her head. The day was warm and sunny. The men were taking the corn out of the fields and unloading it in the rick-yard just behind the farm-house. It was all going according to plan, just as it had been at Mickleditch, save that the Flambards wagons were rather more rickety and the horses a wearier breed. Dick was supervising the rick-building, standing up in the middle of the layered traves with a pitchfork, Stanley beside him. Wilhelm was pitching up and Tizzy was sitting on one of the cart-horses, waiting to take them back to the field. When he saw Mark and Christina he turned and waved, full of excitement, and shouted something to Dick. Christina saw Dick toss a trave down into place, very deliberately, and then stand waiting. The rick was half built, and Dick looked down on them as they came to a halt beside the wagon. Christina was glad about this small physical point, remembering Dick on the ground, tightening Treasure's girths for Mark, and Mark looking down on him.

'That's a new horse!' Tizzy called out. 'Where d'you get him? Is he your horse? Can I have a ride?'

'He's Mr. Masters's horse.' Mark's eyes went past Tizzy and rested on Dick. He gave a curt nod.

'Good morning, sir.' Dick's voice was expressionless.

The last time they had met, seven years ago, he had beaten Mark into unconsciousness. There was nothing in his face to give anything away, the eyes very blue, narrowed against the sun.

'Can I have a ride?' Tizzy had slithered off Ginger's broad back and was looking eagerly up at Mark. 'Will you give me a ride? She won' let me ride Pheasan'. She never will.' He gave Christina his indignant glare. Mark looked down on him, grinning.

'She won't let you ride Pheasant? Why not?'

'Because he's not fit for a six-year-old,' Christina put in quickly. 'He's very funny-tempered. Ask Fowler. Fowler can't do anything with him. That's why I got him so cheaply.'

Mark looked at her with a faint derision in his eyes. 'You mean no one can ride him but you? Not even your ex-cavalry man here?' He jerked his head in Dick's direction.

'Dick has never tried him. He works here on the farm, not as a groom.' Christina's voice was sharp.

'Can I have a ride?' Tizzy insisted.

Mark leaned down from the saddle and pulled Tizzy up in front of him on the big chestnut.

'Can we canter?' Tizzy was wriggling with excitement.

'Why not?'

Christina looked uncertainly at Dick, and saw that the expression had come back into his eyes. He was watching Tizzy's display of admiration and affection for Mark with his feelings written quite plainly on his face. She had always

117

guessed that he loved Tizzy dearly, although he had never made
any obvious gestures to indicate the fact; now was the first time
Christina had seen it proved. His expression moved her to
despair, and she knew perfectly well that she could do nothing
about it. She saw Mark nudge the chestnut with his heels and
start moving away towards the gate. Dick started to work again,
calling down to Wilhelm to carry on pitching. He did not look
at Christina.

Christina followed Mark and when Hannibal started to
canter she put Pheasant into a canter, too, and followed them
up the cart-track beside the stubble. She sat still and tight in
the saddle, holding Pheasant's eager mouth, her feelings in a
turmoil.

Tizzy had lunch in the house and was in no hurry to go back
to the fields. He sat with his elbows on the table, listening to
Mark's story of skirmishes with the Turks, the evacuation of
Suvla Bay and of riding across the Sinai Desert. Christina,
whose geography was vague, acceded that there was possibly
good reason that they had not heard from Mark. He had been
reported missing after fighting near Gaza, where he was taken
prisoner; later the prison camp had been retaken by the Allies,
and Mark had been repatriated. He obviously liked Army life;
he was physically very hard, and mentally callous enough to be
unaffected by the suffering involved. He had no nerves, as
Christina knew from their hunting days. Tizzy was entranced.

'Go along,' Christina chided him at last. 'What will Wilhelm
do without you to lead the horses?'

'I don't like seeing that Hun b—— on my land,' Mark said,
picking up the reference to Wilhelm.

'We wouldn't have anything to harvest if it hadn't been for
him,' Christina said. 'He's a marvellous worker.' She decided
to change the subject. 'Does Dorothy know you're still around?'

'Dorothy? No, I don't suppose so.'

'She wrote not long ago, and asked after you.'

'Did she now?' Mark grinned, and eyed Christina thoughtfully. 'You match-making?'

'I wouldn't have thought you needed anyone for that. It's
just that you're so bad at writing letters, I thought—if you
haven't bothered to tell her you're still alive—'

'She ought to know? A good point. She's all right, is Dorothy.'

Mark tilted his chair back and yawned. 'What is there to do—apart from writing letters? Come for a ride?'

'There's plenty of work out in the fields. I shall go up there this afternoon and help. I usually work up there all day.'

'Making eyes at Dick?'

Christina did not reply. Mark tilted his chair again, and laughed.

Chapter 11

Tizzy was riding Hannibal round the park. Christina watched from her sitting-room window, frowning. Tizzy looked tiny on the big horse—lonely, Christina thought—steering it with intense concentration in a big circle round Mark, who stood shouting at him, slapping a cane into a patch of thistles, impatient as ever at standing still. Tizzy was excited, and frightened, too—not so much frightened of Hannibal as of disappointing his impatient instructor. Christina, from her own experience, knew that Mark was an abominable teacher, intolerant and scornful.

'If he is going to be taught at all, Dick is the person to teach him,' Christina said to Isobel. Isobel grinned at her, swaying drunkenly from her seat on the floor. Isobel was brown and firm and fat, all smiles. Christina could not understand how so much contentment could have been born out of a year of such agonizing misery: not a mark of it had been left on the baby. Every time she looked at her, even now, Christina wanted to laugh, and forget all the things she had to worry about. She lifted Isobel and held her up in the air, waggling her so that the baby laughed out loud, all waving arms and legs.

'Phew! You're a heavyweight! Hannibal will be just your mark when you start riding, tubby!'

Mark loved Isobel, too, with a careless, demonstrative affection that made the baby's face light up every time she saw him. Christina was torn by these conflicting relationships: there were so many reasons why it would be a good thing if she were to marry Mark. When Isobel laughed, and Tizzy adored, she almost forgot the other side of Mark, the inconsistency, the cruelty. She had to make herself remember that the children would grow up, and would no longer amuse Mark when they wanted to do things he did not approve of, and then he would be as intolerant as old Russell had been. Isobel and Tizzy wouldn't laugh then. Already Tizzy, with his Rotherhithe instinct for self-preservation, had discovered that Mark was not invariably approving. Christina had seen the first flicker of astonishment in his eyes one morning when Mark woke up with a hangover and returned Tizzy's devotion with a sharp clip on the ear and a quite unjustified reprimand.

Christina was finding the situation in the house something of a strain, and it showed in her face. The legal tangles did nothing to help either. The first session with Perkins showed that she now owned nothing, save her money and her daughter. There might even be some doubt about her claim on Tizzy, if Mark chose to dispute it and make Tizzy his heir. Mark owned every brick and every sod of Flambards, even including the corn crop that was now harvested and stacked in perfect order down in the rick-yard.

Christina put Isobel down on the floor again, and opened the door to the scratching of Marigold, who visited her occasionally when she wanted a rest from her puppies. There were six of them, and they lived in the kitchen. Mark called them the Flambards pack. 'We'll keep every one of 'em, and hunt them ourselves as soon as this ruddy war is finished.' The bitch came in, followed Christina to the sofa and laid her muzzle on Christina's lap. Christina caressed the floppy ears thoughtfully.

If only there was somewhere she could go to, she was thinking, she would go. But there wasn't. Mark had another month of leave still due to him, and in another month Christina thought she would go mad. She could not sleep, worrying over the future; while Mark's presence in the house seemed to infect the whole place with his own restlessness. Tizzy no longer took any interest in what went on on the farm; Christina, with a larger household to feed and look after, rarely had time to ride out and see what was happening. She thought of Dick constantly; his face as he had watched Tizzy ride away with Mark haunted her. She knew now that—apart from the children—Dick was the only person in her life whom she cared for. She did not want him to be hurt, and he was hurt. She could do nothing about it.

She spent the afternoon doing chores at her desk and watching Isobel, then went into the kitchen to make the customary pot of tea for Mark. Mary was baking; the smell of pastry and bread was wafting out of the open door and windows; a wasp droned over an open jampot.

'Oh, ma'am, I think you'd better come!' Fowler appeared at the kitchen door, panting, all agitation. 'It's young Tizzy—he—' Fowler could not get his breath.

'What is it? What's wrong?'

'He—he went for a ride on Pheasant, ma'am, and now the horse has come back without him.'

'He *what*?' Christina's voice shook with anger. 'He took Pheasant?' She knew instantly what had happened. 'He asked Mark? And Mark let him! Is that it?'

'I wouldn't know, ma'am, but I dare say you're right. Mr. Mark has gone to look for him on Hannibal.'

'How long has Pheasant been back? Watch Isobel, Mary—I must go and see what's happening. Has he just come back?'

'No, ma'am, he's been back nearly an hour. That's why I came to fetch you. The lad would be back now if he'd come to no harm.'

'Oh!' Christina was shaking with rage. Only Mark could do this to her, set her boiling with indignation; her anger with Mark was greater than her fear for Tizzy. 'Why didn't you stop him? You *knew*—'

'I wasn't there, ma'am, else you know I'd have tried. But with Mr. Mark you never can tell him much—'

'The *fool*! The fool—' She remembered, with a cold spasm in her stomach, how Mark had made her ride Treasure when she was just learning to ride, and how Treasure had taken off with her. She remembered his terrifying strength; she saw Pheasant's strength flooding thin Tizzy, and the brightness of fear in Tizzy's eyes. She remembered the incident vividly, as if it had happened an hour ago.

'Did Mark say which way Pheasant went?'

'Through the covert, ma'am.'

'Put my saddle on Pheasant and I'll ride out. And go and tell the boys to look over on the other side. I'll go down the ride and find Mark and see where he's looked already. It's no good us all going to the same place.'

She waited impatiently while Fowler got Pheasant, trying to make herself believe that Mark was already on his way back with Tizzy. But there was no comforting thud of hoofs to be heard, only the skylarks twittering over the home fields and the woodpigeons calling from the covert. The late afternoon sun was warm, some sparrows were taking a dust-bath in the doorway of the hayshed: hard to make one believe that there was anything wrong. But as she waited Christina was conscious of the sort of fear she had once felt for Will, a clammy, sick impatience that needled her into action. She paced backwards and forwards, and went to fetch Pheasant while Fowler was still girthing him up.

'Damned horse,' Fowler muttered.

'Blame Mark, not Pheasant,' Christina said shortly.

She mounted from the block and went out of the yard at a canter, across the wide home fields. The horse was easy and bold, unaware of his sins, raking out with the smooth stride that Tizzy must have loved—until he found he was not its master. He would have been back immediately if he had not been hurt; he would have been all excitement, his brown gipsy face lifted with pride at achieving his great ambition in life. 'Little devil—' He would have known that it was wrong, and Mark would have laughed and urged him on, pleased with the child's courage. Mark had never known prudence.

'Where did you take him, Pheasant? What did you do with him?'

She thought Pheasant would probably have gone down to the farm, out of habit, for he often got a feed in a loose-box down there, when Christina stayed to do some work. But then, surely, the boys must have seen him? When she got to the covert she pulled Pheasant up and went into the shady ride at a walk. A jay flashed across the path, shrieking, then there was silence, the deep, waiting silence that is peculiar to thick woodland. Far away, the sun was still shining. Christina stopped.

'What have you done with him?'

Pheasant twitched back an ear, and shook his head against the bit. Christina felt anxiety biting, her hands cold, her heart thudding into the silence. She could not bear to face what might have happened. 'Not after everything else,' she thought. 'Not Tizzy.' She would not let it into her mind, nudging

Pheasant forward to break the desolate silence, to hear his hoofs on the peat and the twigs breaking. It was no good thinking. The stillness of the covert was terrible.

'Up, Pheasant, come on!'

She trotted quickly on into the ride and then cantered, the panic rising, the images pressing into her mind. She wanted Dick, and then she would look for Tizzy. She could not wander through the golden evening with her brain trembling, teeming with these awful pictures. She had been brave enough over Will, but now there didn't seem to be anything left; she felt that calm and reason were qualities she now knew nothing of. She wanted Dick's calm desperately.

Pheasant came out of the covert into the barley stubble, and Christina saw Dick and Wilhelm in the bottom field, each of them marked by the trail of turned earth behind their horses. She had not even been aware that they had started ploughing. The first furrows gave her a jerk of surprise. She urged Pheasant on and went down over the stubble at a gallop.

'What's the matter? What's wrong?'

Dick had pulled his horses up and was waiting, leaning on the plough handles.

'Oh, Dick, it's Tizzy!' Christina explained what had happened, holding Pheasant in as he pranced round the stolid farm-horses.

'Will you come and help look for him? Mark is out looking, but I'm sure the whole thing is just a joke to him. And if the boys aren't doing anything, perhaps they could come? It will be going dusk before long—he could be lying anywhere.'

Dick straightened up, not making any comment. Christina sensed his restraint, the distance between them that had grown so disastrously since Mark had come back. But his merely being there made her feel very much better, as if everything was under control again. He turned and shouted something to Wilhelm, who was coming back down his stretch some fifty yards away, then he took one of his plough-horses out of the traces and stripped it of its harness, save for the bridle, and mounted it with an apparently simple vault. Even a plough-horse would canter for Dick. Christina was charmed, in spite of her distress, to see it go ahead of her up the field, Dick sitting easily, one hand dangling by its side, one on its neck. Pheasant caught him up, and they cantered together, and Dick turned and smiled at Christina.

'Don't worry! Tizzy is tough. It'll show him you weren't warning him off for nothing.'

'Mark should have known! It's not as if I haven't told him—Fowler told him, too.'

Dick did not reply, his opinion of Mark too well known to need reiterating.

As they went back into the covert they saw Mark coming down the ride on Hannibal. He looked worried, and Christina immediately sensed that all differences would be forgotten until Tizzy was found. He even looked slightly remorseful, which made Christina feel worse than if he had been cocky.

'I can't understand where he can have got to. Pheasant came this way, the last I saw of him—although I suppose he could have taken any of the rides.'

'He didn't come out this side, else we'd have seen him,' Dick said.

'No—well, I suppose he could have circled round and back into the home fields, or even gone out towards Hall Farm, through the Lower Wood. Tizzy might have managed to steer him a bit before he fell off.'

Christina thought of the tangled undergrowth and over-grown tracks through the Lower Wood, and her fear jerked again. They separated and each took a track out into the neglected fingers of the covert, looking for hoof-prints. Mark had searched all the obvious places, and the fields between the stables and the woods. Pheasant went innocently, playing with his bit, bored now with all this standing and walking. Far above their heads the trees bowed and tossed in the evening breeze and wisps of cloud were glowing pink with the fading sun, but in the wood it was sombre and close.

'Tizzy! Tizzy!' Their voices echoed, and the pigeons wheeled up. Christina's mind began to linger on the possibilities again, so that she started to shiver until a sharp whistle from somewhere ahead made her pull herself together. She called out, and the whistle replied. She put Pheasant into a trot, ducking to avoid the branches.

'Over here!'

Pheasant came out into a clearing, and Christina saw Dick's plough-horse grazing.

'Dick! Where are you?'

'He's here!' Dick's voice came from the trees across the gap. Christina cantered across the grass and Dick came out of the trees with Tizzy in his arms.

'Is he all right?'

Tizzy was conscious, but looked very strange—un-Tizzy-like, Christina thought. She was shocked by the wandering of his eyes, and the fact that they looked at her and seemed to register nothing. He did not say anything, and his eyes went to Dick without any expression, and up to the trees, and he smiled.

'Tiger ran away and hit a brick wall,' he said. 'Charlie was mad.'

'Oh, Dick!' Christina was petrified. 'What's wrong with him?'

'He's had a bang on the head. Don't worry. He's wandering a bit. He seems all right otherwise. He needs a good rest, then he'll wake up with a headache, but that's all.'

'Are you sure?'

'Yes. I've seen it dozens of times. A spot of concussion.'

Tizzy's skin, in spite of the sunburn, had a ghastly greenish cast. Christina let out her breath in a sharp sigh. 'Oh, I wouldn't know—I'm glad you're here . . . I couldn't . . .' She could feel herself shaking, feeble as Tizzy. She despised herself, and the effort it took her not to cry.

'It's all right, Christina,' Dick said.

She led the horses, and Dick went ahead with Tizzy. She thought, 'Dick is no longer just a farm-hand for me. Everything has changed.' She thought now that all the time she was asking Dick what to do, depending on him, and not just for when to start ploughing, and when to turn the hay. It was for everything, even Tizzy's health. She could not help it.

They could not find Mark, although they called, and did not meet him until they were almost home, half-way across the last field. He cantered across to them, reining in sharply.

'Is he all right?'

'A bang on the head,' Dick said. 'That's all.'

'God, that's a fool horse of yours, Christina. There was nothing to make him take off like that.'

'I told you he was like that,' Christina said. 'You knew.' She could feel herself shaking with the effort to keep her temper.

'It needs a spot of discipline. I'll give it some schooling to-morrow.'

'You won't,' Christina said.

Mark's face tightened. He said to Dick, 'I'll take Tizzy now. You can go back to the farm.'

Dick stopped and faced Mark. 'I'll put Mrs. Russell's horse away for her, and I'll go and fetch Dr. Porter, if you'll let me ride the chestnut. Someone will have to fetch him.'

Mark hesitated. Then he swung himself out of the saddle and said, 'Very well, if you can't manage the bay.'

Dick opened his mouth to say something, then shut it firmly, his eyes glinting. Mark took Tizzy from him. Christina watched them, aware of the tension, biting her lip. Mark gave Dick Hannibal's reins, and Dick took the other two horses from Christina and set off towards the stable without saying anything else. Christina followed Mark, still biting her lip to stop herself from saying all the things that raged through her mind.

Seeing to Tizzy distracted her as soon as they got to the house, and Mark said no more to exacerbate her feelings, making for the whisky bottle as soon as he had laid Tizzy on the bed in Will's room, where Christina had been obliged to move Tizzy while Mark was on leave. Tizzy was barely conscious as Christina undressed him, but his thin, wiry body was unmarked, save for the lump on the back of his head. 'Thank God,' Christina thought, unable to contemplate a child's pain. 'He might have killed you, my little hedgehog.' And by 'he' she meant Mark, not Pheasant. Tizzy's eyes opened once and he looked at her and said, 'Ma, I rode him.'

'Yes, you rode him, and see where it got you!' But she was relieved by the fact that he knew her, and his colour was improving.

Dr. Porter came, shown up by Mary, and examined Tizzy carefully. Christina stood by the window, looking out into the dusk. Across the park she saw a shadow moving, a fitful, uneasy shadow against the darkness of the trees. She watched it carefully, recognizing her own horse, and Dick riding him. Her eyes widened with surprise, but she felt a warmth, not anger. Dick was not going to let Pheasant get away with his day's work, but he would not break him as Mark would break him; he would defeat him by patience, which Mark knew nothing of. Christina's eyes followed him, forgetting Tizzy. She was very much aware of her own feelings, no longer surprised by them. She just wanted to watch Dick, even the faint, distant shadow of him which merely told her that he was there, no more. She started when Dr. Porter spoke to her.

'Concussion,' he said. 'There's nothing else. He must rest. I'll come again in the morning and look at him, but I don't think you've anything to worry about. He'll be as right as rain after a good night's sleep.'

'Thank goodness! I was frightened—'

'You Russells and your horses—you ought to be used to it by now. Young Dick is looking a lot better than when he came, I'm pleased to see.'

'Yes.' Christina was cautious. Had her thoughts been so apparent, that Dr. Porter had mentioned Dick? But his old voice bumbled on: 'That child . . . I've never seen a boy so like his father. It doesn't seem any time at all since it was Mark's broken nose—the time that roan mare fell with him. And now this little monkey—just the same . . .'

Dr. Porter had tended three generations of Russells, helped them either to die or be born, and tidied them up after their horses had thrown them: he was entitled to speak with familiarity. Nobody else outside the family had ever mentioned Tizzy's father.

'I'll call in the morning.'

'Thank you.' Christina saw him out; the park was still and silent now, lit by a harvest moon. Christina stood on the doorstep, shivering, filled with these strange emotions. Mary came to shut the door, thinking it had been left open, and grumbled when she saw Christina.

'Keep the warm in now, Miss Christina. Like as not we'll be up tonight with young Tizzy. These evenings are drawing in . . . I've lit a fire for Mr. Mark.'

'Will you keep an eye on Tizzy for a few minutes?' Christina said. 'I shan't be long.'

'Very well. Oh, and by the way, ma'am, I meant to tell you— a telegram came from Mr. Perkins this afternoon, to say he was calling here tomorrow.'

'Mr. Perkins? Oh, the solicitor. Very well. Does Mark know?'

'Yes, ma'am.'

If Mr. Perkins could resolve their problems he would be a very clever man.

Christina fetched an old coat off its peg, wrapped it round her shoulders and went quietly out of the front door. She walked down to the stables and saw the lantern lit, hanging on its hook, throwing gigantic shadows on the whitewashed brick. A horse's head moved, and a hand soothed it; there was the clink of a feed-bucket and the eager, fluttering noise in Pheasant's nostrils as he waited greedily. Christina was smiling. She stood inside the doorway and watched Dick tip the feed in the horse's manger. He had been rubbing Pheasant down and was in his shirt-sleeves. His cap hung on the partition, his pale hair gleamed in the lantern-light.

'Dick.'

He turned round, very surprised, and instantly guarded. Christina saw his face; she saw the wariness, but she had seen the expression that it replaced.

'I came to tell you—' But there was only one thing she wanted to tell him, and she stopped pretending that she had come to tell him about Tizzy, or ask him about Pheasant, and went up to him. 'Dick, I—'

He dropped the feed-bucket and put his arms round her, very gently.

'Yes,' she said, 'I came to tell you—' She buried her face in his white shirt and her arms went up round his shoulders.

'I love you,' he said.

'Yes.'

'Ever since I was fifteen. I have loved you since then.'

'Yes, I came—I wanted you. I had to come.'

He said her name, and kissed her. Christina had no misgivings at all, but was filled with a sense of relief, as if she had come to an even keel, as if she had come into daylight out of a deep fog. She did not know whether to laugh or cry. This was not love as she had known it for Will, but, whatever its name, she felt it was based on rock. This feeling of strength in Dick was what she remembered about the first time he had held her in his arms; it had not changed at all. She felt the hardness of his body under his shirt, the smell of horses and earth in their breathing, his pale hair beneath her fingers.

'Dick—'

Pheasant finished his feed and looked for his hay, but there was none there. He turned and nibbled Dick's cap until it fell in the straw, then pushed at Dick's elbow. Christina laughed. They got Pheasant his hay, and Dick led the plough-horse out into the yard. The orange October moon hung low, on its back, washing the familiar yard with a radiant light.

'Tizzy is all right,' Christina remembered. 'Dr. Porter said he will be his old self tomorrow.'

'Is that what you came to tell me?'

'I saw you riding Pheasant in the park. I couldn't stop watching you. I had to come.'

Dick grinned. 'God, I wouldn't mind taking him out again! Or ploughing all through the night. I don't feel like going to sleep!'

'You will by the time you've ridden that beast home! You'll never get him to canter again.'

'Oh, I could make him jump a five-barred gate the way I feel. You're all right, Christina—with Mark, I mean? Do you want me to come back with you? He doesn't bully you, does he?'

'Oh, Mark—' Christina shrugged, remembering the things that were unresolved. 'No. I'm all right. I don't hide anything from Mark. He must just make the best of it.'

But Mark didn't have to know, she thought, with a small tremor of apprehension. What had happened tonight did not change anything. It had been happening all the time. She did not have to burst in and say, 'I love Dick.'

Dick kissed her again, standing beside the patient horse. Then he vaulted on, in spite of the fact that the mounting-block was right behind him, and Christina walked with him to the gate out into the field.

'Good night!'

'Did you say this old horse wouldn't gallop?' Dick said softly.

And the Suffolk Punch went off with a grunt and a sharp flick of his docked tail, his great hoofs pounding the track as he raced for the covert, Dick's ardour inspiring him so that he looked for all the world like one of his ancestors at Agincourt, clods flying and blinkers flapping. Christina stood and laughed. She was in a dream. She walked home, not thinking about anything, the old coat trailing from her shoulders.

'Wherever have you been? You must be starving,' Mary said peevishly as she went in at the kitchen door.

Christina realized that she was.

'Why, has Mark eaten? I hope you didn't wait.'

'No. Mr. Mark's had his. He's gone up to Tizzy. I'll heat yours up—give me ten minutes.'

'I'll go and get washed.'

She went up to her room. She heard Tizzy laughing, and was annoyed, remembering that he was supposed to be sleeping. She went into Will's room and saw him sitting up in bed, his eyes very bright, while Mark sat beside him, telling him about the day Treasure had run away with her.

' "Stop, stop!" she screamed!'

'Oh, Mark, really! He's supposed to be getting plenty of rest. Leave him alone and let him sleep. You'll get him all worked up.'

Mark looked up carelessly. 'Oh, all right. I was just telling him that it doesn't matter. He'll be riding again tomorrow, won't you, my lad? You'll get the better of that wild animal of Christina's!'

The excitement left Tizzy's face and he looked at Mark with a strange expression on his face. Christina saw a pretence at eagerness and, underneath it, stark fear. He murmured something inaudible.

'You must never let them beat you,' Mark said easily. 'They don't let you get away with it in the Army, you know. They keep you at it, even if you're half dead. That's the way to become a rider, Tizzy. Never give in.'

'No,' said Tizzy. His eyes met Christina's with a mute, trembling plea.

Mark got up. 'We'll have you on him again in the morning. You have a good rest now, and you'll be as right as rain. I've had more knocks like that than I can remember and it's done me no harm.'

Christina, biting back the rage yet again, resisted her passion to speak and tucked in Tizzy's sheets. Mark went to the door and said to her, 'Where've you been?' Christina did not reply. She said softly to Tizzy, 'Go to sleep now, sweetheart. Don't think about horses. Don't worry. I won't let you ride Pheasant again.'

She heard Mark go away down the landing. She kissed Tizzy gently. Tizzy looked at her with anxious eyes.

'He says I must ride him again. I must ride him again!'

'No. Mark isn't right about everything.'

'He *is* right!'

'Pheasant is my horse, whatever Mark says. And I say you must not ride him.'

Tizzy's eyes looked at her doubtfully.

'He *is* right about everything.'

'All right, he is. But Pheasant is mine, and I won't let you ride him.'

The tautness went out of Tizzy's face. 'You're sure you won't let me?'

'Yes.'

'I won't have to?'

'No.'

Tizzy sighed, and shut his eyes. Christina sat by the bed watching him, a hard knot of compassion for him filling in her throat. Being Mark's son was no easy matter, just as being his father's son had been no easy matter for Will. She could see it happening all over again, and remembered clearly how Will had suffered in the very same way, scorned for not being able to negotiate a fearful hedge. Will's life with his father had been acutely unhappy. And Tizzy now was finding that the Russell path was not all roses.

She sat with him until he was sleeping soundly, and then she went downstairs. She ate her supper in the kitchen with just Mary for company, letting the old woman's flow of comment on the day's work ride over her, listening to the scolding and the dismay and the conjecture, and not thinking about it at all. Thinking about Dick. Mary washed up and tidied the kitchen, and Christina sat on.

'I'll go to bed now, ma'am.'

'Very well. Thank you, Mary.'

'Will you be joining Mr. Mark in the sitting-room, ma'am? Then I can put the lamps out.'

'No. I'll put them out.'

Mary gave her a strange look, and sniffed. 'Very well. Good night, ma'am.'

'Good night.'

Christina wanted to be alone. She did not want to talk, or even think, but just sit looking into the fire. She did not know what was going to happen: she just knew that she felt very happy, after what felt like a very long time. And she had no feelings of guilt or compunction about Will; she loved Will no less, nor ever would. He was a part of her, a part of the person Dick loved, a part of everything. It all made perfect sense, just at that moment.

But her reverie was interrupted by Mark. He came into the kitchen to get some water for his whisky, and was startled to see Christina sitting by the range, doing nothing.

'I thought you'd gone to bed,' he said. 'Why the solitude?'

He went into the scullery and topped up his glass. Christina could see that he had drunk a good deal already.

'I'm just going,' she said, getting to her feet. She did not wish to discuss anything with Mark.

'Are you avoiding me? I'm in disgrace, I suppose?'

'Let's not talk about it.'

'Have a drink, Christina. I'll fetch you one. You're such a strait-laced female. Do you never see the funny side of things?'

'Not of putting Tizzy on Pheasant, no. I don't want a drink, thank you.'

'What's wrong with you? What are you hatching, sitting here in the dark?'

'Nothing.'

'Where did you get to just now? When you didn't come down for supper? I thought you were with Tizzy, and Mary said you'd gone out.'

Christina did not reply. She did not want her feelings lacerated by Mark, not tonight. She turned and made for the open door.

'Not so fast!' Mark was across the room in a flash, and took her by the arm. 'You're my guest in this house, Christina. I want to talk to you.'

Exasperated, Christina shook his hand off. 'I'll talk to you when your head's clear. I don't want to discuss what you did today—I've been very careful not to say a word! You must know what I think of the whole business. Or do you want me to tell you?' She changed her mind, stung by his persistence. 'I will if that's what you want—Pheasant is *my* horse, and Tizzy is by law *my* child—not yours, and I told you quite clearly, and so did Fowler, that Pheasant is a dangerous horse for anyone but me to ride, and you could well have killed Tizzy doing what you did this afternoon. And am I supposed to laugh? Where is the funny side to that? You tell me.'

'You haven't answered my question,' said Mark quietly.

'What question?'

'Where were you just now?'

'What has that to do with it?'

'Why won't you tell me?'

'I'm not answerable to you for every minute of the day.'

'I know why you won't tell me. You were with Dick, weren't you?'

'Yes.'

'What is he to you? Just a man you employ?'

Christina hesitated. 'What right have you to ask me that?'

'I've every right in the world. You're my brother's wife, a Russell, and Russells don't stoop to rolling in the hay with farm-labourers.'

Christina's eyes widened abruptly, her calm shattered by Mark's argument, the most preposterous of any he might have thought up. 'What about you and Violet? What's the difference, if that's the way you look at it?' she asked him sharply.

'Oh, don't be stupid, Christina.'

'It was nothing to you, but it was everything in the world to Violet, and you never gave her another thought.'

'You're off the point—we were talking about Dick. What is there between you?' Mark's face was flushed, and his eyes glittered with drink and growing anger.

'I love him, if you want to know.' Christina threw prudence to the winds, incensed by Mark's attitude. 'It's perfectly simple.'

134

'You're not such a fool!' Mark's anger exploded. 'You must be out of your mind—'

'I've never been saner in my life.'

'Dick is a peasant, you stupid woman! What does he possess, apart from the clothes he stands up in? He's just an opportunist, after your money—'

'Like you, I suppose! You're not my guardian, Mark, to say who I may like and who I may not! And Dick is no more a peasant than—'

'He's dirt, Christina, and you know it. Tomorrow I shall send him packing—I shall kick him out—'

'Then I shall go, too!' Christina's voice shook, pure rage crowding out dismay. 'And your precious place will rot to pieces, and much good it will do you! You've never raised a finger to *work* since the day you were born, but you still expect to have horses and servants and think you're the squire, to tell everyone how they should behave—'

'Yes, I'm still the master in this house, and don't you forget it.' Mark straightened up, his eyes very hard and scornful. 'I'm sorry if I upset your plans by turning up again, just when you—'

'Don't worry! Flambards means very little to me. I shall leave in the morning, and your farm can go back to being a wilderness for all I care—'

'And where will you go to?' Mark taunted her. 'Tell me that.'

'I shall go down to the cottage.'

'To your peasant!'

'No! Dick will have gone—haven't you just said that yourself?' Christina's voice spat with a rage that was scarcely under control. The mockery in Mark's face incensed her, and she no longer cared how wild her plans were in her passion to be rid of him. 'I shall stay there—and pay you rent—until I have found somewhere else to live.'

'Very suitable! You will find out what it's like to live like a peasant, as you're so addicted to the breed.'

'I shall take the children. We shan't burden you by our presence another day longer.' Christina heard her voice quiver dangerously. She turned blindly for the door.

'Good. I shall tell Fowler to drive you over first thing in the morning—'

Christina, hardly knowing what she was doing, collided headlong with Tizzy, who was standing on the threshold in his night-shirt.

'Tizzy!'

'I wan' a drink.'

'Oh, Tizzy, what are you doing here? You're supposed to be asleep! Come up with me, you little idiot child! I'll get you a drink.'

She picked him up and carried him up the passage and across the hall, still seething against Mark, but wrenched by concern for Tizzy. He was too heavy to carry up the stairs, and she put him down gently and put her arm round him.

'I don't want to go to the farm,' he said. 'I won't go away.'

'Hush, Tizzy. Come on now, back to bed.'

'I'm not going away.'

'No.'

'I'm staying here. I'm not—'

'It doesn't concern you, Tizzy. Come along and get your drink.'

'I'm not going.'

'For heaven's sake, Tizzy!'

Christina felt her patience giving way. Her head was whirling. She tucked Tizzy into bed again and got him a drink. His colour was good and he was not feverish. He seemed perfectly recovered from his fall. 'Thank goodness!' she breathed. There was enough to worry about now, without Tizzy.

'All right now?'

'Yes.'

She kissed him, and went into her own room. Isobel lay with her plump brown arms thrown up on the pillow, fingers curled, dark lashes like ink lines on the perfect skin. Christina looked at her in an agony of indecision, seeing nothing but the awful responsibility she represented. She could hear her own pulses thudding in the stillness of her room, the blood racing with a furious indignation which—even in her lifelong battles with Mark—she had never experienced to the same degree. She felt as shaken, lacerated, as if she had been in physical conflict. She walked about the room, the conversation repeating itself with all its venomous accusations over and over in her head. She stood at the dressing-table and tore the hairpins out of her hair and saw the hot tears of self-pity brimming under her eyelids, cursed herself for a fool, and paced back to the window, cooling her forehead against the glass, seeing nothing of the moon and the windy October night. The draughts rattled through the window-frames, and she shivered and turned away.

'I shall never sleep!' she thought. The day behind her was a great, ravening pattern of worry, fear, ecstasy, and rage: she did not know how she could ever find peace with so much emotion rampaging through her bloodstream. But she undressed and got into bed, and lay looking at the cracks on the ceiling, traced out by the moonlight which came and went through the passing clouds.

'I've had enough,' she thought. 'I cannot think any more.'

The day seemed to have gone on for ever.

Chapter 12

Christina slept, when sleep came, very heavily. She did not know what woke her, but she felt instantly, as soon as she opened her eyes, that something was wrong. She looked towards the window, saw that it was just going light, and remembered the argument of the night before.

'Oh, God!'

She did not want to leave Flambards, for all she had said. Her head ached miserably.

She lay still, looking at the grey sky, and the feeling of uneasiness came again. She got out of bed, put on her dressing-gown and went across the passage to Tizzy's room. His bed was empty. She stood looking at it blankly, not sure what it meant. Then she noticed that his clothes weren't there.

A feeling of intense irritation, rather than of anxiety, flared up to augment her general misery. Tizzy did not get up as early as this as a rule, even when he was fit. Was he wandering about somewhere in a daze, or had he been upset by the fierce argument he had overheard the evening before? Or merely gone down to feed the horses with Fowler?

Christina got dressed, and went down to the kitchen. It was empty. She went outside, into a grey, tossing, miserable morning, very well suited to her mood, and explored the park and the stables. Fowler, just arrived on his bicycle, had not seen Tizzy.

'Well, now, the little devil! What's he up to, then?'

'He must have gone to the farm. There's nowhere else he can be.'

But why, Christina wondered? Had he gone to look for Dick, to find comfort after yesterday's violence? Even Tizzy must have found by now that Dick was a more reliable oracle than Mark. She knew she would not be able to rest until she knew where he was. But if she went down to the farm now she knew the interpretation that Mark would put on the outing.

'I shall have to tell Mark what's happened,' she thought. 'The whole business is his fault. He can do a bit of the worrying, too.'

And then she realized that Tizzy might be with Mark. She had never thought to look in Mark's room.

She hurried back to the house and up to Mark's room. Mark was still in bed, lying with his hands clasped behind his head.

'Have you seen Tizzy this morning?'

'No.'

'He's disappeared. I've looked everywhere.'

Mark frowned. With his rumpled black hair, Palestinian suntan, and the gold identity disc on a chain round his neck, he looked like a foreigner. 'What are you worried about?' he said. 'He'll just have gone out to look at Pheasant or something.'

'He's not in the stables. I thought he might have gone up to the farm. I want to go and look, but I want you to know what I've gone for. He's in no state to be wandering about on his own. Dr. Porter said he must stay in bed.'

Mark grinned. 'Go and look, then. You might even see Dick while you're up there.'

Christina went out of the room, slamming the door, biting down the familiar rage. They still reacted on each other exactly as they had all through their childhood, baiting and nagging, with last night's affair the grand culmination of all their years of practice. Christina was amazed that she still rose to his goading, but she could not help herself. She had no more self-control than an adolescent girl teased by an elder brother.

She did not tell Mary what had happened, not wanting her to fuss. She told her to leave Tizzy and just attend to Isobel. Then she went out to get Pheasant. Soon she was cantering through the damp covert, cross and confused, her thoughts in a tangle.

She did not particularly want to see Dick until she had pulled herself together, but she knew finding Tizzy would go a good way to calming her state of mind. It was a bleak morning, a cold drizzle slanting across grey fields.

Half-way through the covert she got her first whiff of wood-smoke, which surprised her. She knew the boys had not started hedging, and there could be no other explanation for the smell. It was strong and heavy, rolling towards her on the wind, far too pungent for a mere tramp's brew-up. Coming out of the ride she collected Pheasant for the gallop down the track, and was amazed to see a pall of smoke hanging over the farm. It writhed in the wind, dark and ominous, its core appearing to be in the farm-house itself.

Christina paused, staring. With all the worries she had on her mind, this outside, physical evidence of alarm took several seconds to register.

'Whatever—'

She thought she must be dreaming. Pheasant pulled, reaching for the bit, and the reins slithered through her fingers.

'It can't be on fire!'

But, quite obviously, as a fresh billow of thick smoke rolled low over the track, belching from the doorway of the cottage, it was.

She put Pheasant into a sharp canter, completely alert now, all her other worries forgotten. As they raced down the track she had a forlorn hope that there must be an ordinary explanation for all the smoke-clouds—a mere bonfire, or some fantastic cooking mistake, but as she got near she knew that such ideas were mere illusions: her farm-house was on fire, and burning fast.

She pulled Pheasant to a halt as soon as she felt his uneasiness, feverishly tied up his reins so that he wouldn't tread on them and left him to his own devices. Picking up her skirts, she ran, mud flying.

'Dick! Dick!'

The smoke rolled towards her and then swung round, shredded by the wind into long plumes over the stable-yard. She saw Dick come out of the door of the cottage, ducking low, his hand over his face. He heard her shout and looked up.

'Help me get the horses out,' he said. 'It's got a hold in there.

I tried to stop it, but I can't, and with this wind blowing it could easily spread to the stables.'

He had no breath to waste in talking. Christina could see that he was already affected by the smoke, breathing painfully. Even in the midst of this urgency she felt a great rush of concern for him.

'You're all right, Dick? You—'

'Come on!' he said. 'If only the boys were here—'

He was running into the yard, Christina stumbling after him.

'Dick, have you seen Tizzy?'

He glanced at her with streaming, bloodshot eyes, as if she was stupid. 'No, of course not—'

'He's disappeared.'

Dick shook his head, pulling open the sagging stable door. He had no time for Tizzy. 'They'll be nervous. I'll take Dolly first—she's the quietest. Undo all the head-ropes. With luck they'll all come quietly. Go easy—don't upset them.'

Out of the wind and rain the stable was quiet, yet the horses were stamping uneasily, not bothering about their feeds. The smell of smoke was strong.

'If only the wind were the other way!' Dick said. He went up to Dolly and unfastened her halter-rope. 'Come on, my beauty. Show the others what to do, my pretty.' His voice was soft and caressing. He appeared in no hurry now, very easy, letting her move round in her stall at her own ponderous speed.

'Bring Ginger, Christina. He's easy.'

Christina tried to be very calm like Dick, but her movements were all fumbled with worry, and her voice shaky. Ginger barged her against the partition, almost knocking her off her feet. She could feel his tremors of anxiety, see his eyes—unnaturally large—looking past her for the dangers he could scent. But Dolly's example calmed him. He followed hastily, but without panic. Two more went out, and Christina took the fifth, Dusty. Dick went back for the last, Punch, who was whinnying and stamping his feet. Christina stood at the doorway, watching the pall of smoke twisting in the wind, whirling up into the rain-clouds. She could hear the cracking of burning timbers, and sparks were spitting like bright insects against the sky. The vigour of the fire, fanned by the strong wind, amazed her. The house was built of brick and the roof of slate, yet it was now a shell of fire, enclosed by four walls. Great blasts of heat swept across the low stable roof into her face; the first spark stung her cheek. She saw what Dick meant by the direction of the wind. For the first time she stood and looked at the danger.

'Dick, are you coming?'

She heard Punch whinny again, his hoofs scraping excitedly on the flagged floor. The row of stables was wooden, with bales of hay and straw stacked against the wall nearest to the house. Beyond the stables, and to leeward, stood the rick-yard, with all the season's harvest in neat array, dry as a bone beneath the thatch. Christina, with time to appraise the situation, felt her anxiety harden into real foreboding.

Punch was being difficult, refusing to face up into the direction of the smoke, although that was where the doorway lay. Dick was still easy, his voice quite calm. Christina saw the first flame show above the stable roof as a shower of splitting slates rained down on to the stable tiles. Punch whinnied again.

'Christina!'

She whirled round and saw Mark riding into the yard on Hannibal. Dick came to the doorway at the same moment, swearing softly.

'Have you got a scarf?' he asked Christina. 'The damned animal is going to fry at this rate.' His eyes went past Christina to Mark and he called out, without a moment's hesitation, 'Can you ride that horse past the doorway, sir? Will he do it?'

Christina swung round. Hannibal was remarkably calm, trusting completely in his rider's judgement of the situation. Mark saw immediately what Dick was about and rode forward. Dick went back to Punch. Christina got out of the way, amazed by this sudden working partnership between the two sworn enemies. They were back in the cavalry again, under fire, literally. Christina saw Mark's concentration, easing the big chestnut into sight of the panic-stricken horse inside, yet aware that only a hair's breadth separated his own horse's trust from panic. Hannibal's eyes were white-rimmed, his ears flitching, listening to Mark's voice, soft and endearing for a change. Mark's hand smoothed his neck.

Punch came out with a rush, almost crushing Dick in the doorway. Hannibal reared up with excitement and swung round, Mark sitting easily, one hand still on the horse's neck.

The animal went off with a bound, but Mark was able to control him and bring him back. He sat in the middle of the yard, watching the fire. Punch had made off, Dick letting him go.

'What started this?' Mark shouted to Dick.

'An armful of straw underneath my bed, with a match thrown in it—while I was out feeding the horses,' Dick shouted back.

Christina gasped, unable to believe her ears. But Mark, aware that discussing the academic question of how the fire started was not the most important job in hand, did not wait to discuss the matter any further. He slipped off Hannibal, threw the reins to Christina and stood watching the fire beside Dick.

'It's starting on the stable now,' Christina heard him say. 'The question is—how to stop it getting the rick-yard?'

'I think, sir, it's a matter of demolishing—'

'The old harness shed? And making a gap?'

'Yes, sir, if we can do it in time. It's pretty rickety.'

'We shall want some help.' Mark turned to Christina. 'Get on that horse and go and round up everyone you can find! As quickly as possible! Else you're going to lose the whole of your harvest.'

He gave her a leg up astride the big chestnut. Christina was away almost before he had finished talking, feeling the blast of heat in her face change to the sting of rain as she hurtled past the disintegrating cottage. She was terrified of the fire's power, writhing and spitting into the gusts of wind, one moment a flattened fan of roaring flame, the next a flaring tower reaching for the sky. It loved the wind, swelling and increasing with every fresh gust. The thin rain did not daunt it.

Her errand was scarcely necessary, for already the village people, having seen the conflagration against the grey morning, were streaming across the fields, anxious not to miss any of the excitement. Stanley was in the vanguard, standing on the pedals of his decrepit bicycle, crashing through the potholes. Everyone was running, even women and children. Christina, having sent a boy on a pony for the fire-brigade (some fifteen miles distant and not really a very optimistic proposition), turned round and galloped back to the farm, and left Hannibal tied to a gate with a piece of baling string, out of the way.

Stanley skidded through the mud behind her, eyes shining.

'Cor, miss, what's Dick been doing?'

'Go and help!' Christina snapped at him. 'Don't just stand and gape.'

The cottage roof had fallen in and the flames had moved over the stable end. Tar ran in bubbling streams down the weatherboard. It was now very hot in the stable-yard, even up against the far buildings. Christina watched, appalled, as the flames roared into the haystore. Burning, filigree hay spun up into the sky, lifted by the conflagration. The sweat ran down Christina's face.

Mark and Dick had fetched a load of tools from the store barn and Mark went out through the gate bawling for volunteers to come and help demolish the sagging end of the stable block.

He gave out sledge-hammers, dispatching one party round the back to attack the tottering walls from the rear.

'Drag all the timber well clear! And hurry!'

The strongest helpers he sent to help Dick, where the heat was already making the work uncomfortable. Little boys were sent for ladders and buckets, and another party for tarpaulins.

'Drag them through the pond—get them soaked through—then go and drape them over the nearest stacks! You boys watch for sparks on the stacks. Go out round the back—hurry! It's the most important job of the lot. Take the ladders, and some sacks to beat with. Wet them first! You go, and Harry, and you over there! Christina, you organize a bucket chain from the pond. The women can do that.'

But the crux of the operation lay in making a gap wide enough to stop the fire from continuing along the block of old sheds that stood at right-angles to the stables, backs to the rick-yard. If that caught, it would be impossible to stop the fire from sweeping across the whole of the rick-yard. Dick had seen the possibilities of the harness shed, the weakest part of the building, but whether it was possible to demolish it before the fire drove them away from the work was doubtful. The least courageous of the volunteers were already making excuses to get away from the heat, but a dogged knot of enthusiasts was flailing away to good effect, knocking out the buttresses that had been put in to support the end wall. With the supports gone, and Dick and Mark using a battering-ram from the inside, the wall started to collapse. Half the roof fell in, raining tiles, and the workers scattered momentarily, then converged once more to attack the sagging rafters and timbers. From the field outside, a working party was dragging the timber clear as soon as it was wrenched loose, and rescuing the heaps of harness that Dick was slinging out through the opening. Sparks rained down on them from the conflagration, lacy confections of burning hay still swarming through the sky, twisting in the wind. Christina had a glimpse of Mark knocking out the side wall with a sledge-hammer, his face running with sweat and blood from a gash where a tile had hit him. Dick and another man were starting on the roof timbers, apparently regardless of danger in the race against the encroaching flames. Another shower of tiles rained down into the yard and a ragged cheer went up as one of the main timbers, after a warning shout from Dick, crashed down on top of the back wall, which collapsed with mortal, splintering shrieks audible even above the din of the flames.

'They're winning!' somebody said.

But the heat was intense. The men clawing away the timber came less readily, ducking and cursing. The fire, having consumed the hay and straw, had shrunk slightly, but its grip was fierce and sure, edging with its greedy roaring and crackling down the whole length of the rotten outside boards of the shed, consuming the wooden partitions and hayracks and roof rafters that stood in its path. Showers of falling tiles would muffle and quench it for mere seconds, then a fresh gust of wind would sweep through its entrails, flicking embers and ash and burning splinters in showers through the yard and over the heads of the frantic workers. The end of the bucket chain could not get within throwing distance of the conflagration. Christina felt the sweat running in rivers down her body, yet she was considerably farther from the flames than the men who worked in its path. She was desperately anxious for Dick, aware that he had forgotten prudence completely, and even concerned to a certain extent for Mark, who had always taken risks readily. They were still closest to the fire, taking out the last section of wall, working close together over one stubborn support that held a whole section from moving. Mark shouted for someone to fetch a chain, and together they fastened it round the top of the baulk and took the end over to their last persevering helpers. A bevy of people, seeing what was needed, crowded in for one desperate effort, and the baulk of timber toppled, freeing a last long section of weatherboarding. But no one would go in to take the timber out; it was too hot. Mark and Dick made a few forays, but were beaten back. Christina saw Dick's face as he turned away, and realized that he was finished, reeling on his feet. A man went up to him and took his arm, supporting him. Christina turned to go after him, but at that moment someone thrust a bucket at her and she realized that Mark had now turned his attention to getting the water moving, and the chain started work, Mark on its end, dousing the fire's path and the dusty floor of what had once been the harness shed.

For the next half-hour there was no thought but for the stomach-wrenching buckets, slopping water, clanking and thudding, across the mire of the yard. The fire was checked, but hung on, flaring up in dangerous gusts as if determined to jump the gap. Mark stationed himself on the corner of the end block, dousing the flames as they darted across, ordering men to beat off every stray brand and ember. So far none of the ricks had been touched, the army of little boys vying with each other to beat out every sailing firebrand that came across. Christina could not see Dick anywhere. She was desperate to know if he was all right, the dreadful ghouls of all the stories of consumption that she had ever heard crowding into her spinning head, all the undoubtedly true facts that she had happily ignored since he had seemed to be getting better fanning into life again like the flames before the wind. And Tizzy! 'Oh, God, Tizzy!' she moaned, grasping yet another slopping bucket in blistered hands. Like everyone else in the yard she was drenched and grimed with smoke, sweat, rain, and mud soaking her clothes, black streaks smearing her cheeks, eyes half closed with smuts and pain.

A shout went up from outside the yard.

'They're coming!'

An unfamiliar noise came on a gust of wind from the direction of the village, a bell jangling with great urgency, neither church nor muffins.

'The fire-brigade!'

'Oh, thank God!'

The little boys started to run with whoops of excitement. Christina dropped her bucket and went across to Mark.

'It will be all right?'

'We've got it beaten, I think. At least they will finish it off for us—I think I've had enough!'

'What's happened to Dick?'

'God knows.' Mark wiped his hand across his face, making a great track through the soot and the blood.

'Oh, Mark, your head!'

'It's thick enough—I never felt it. Let's go and see the captain of this famous fire-brigade. Then I reckon I'm ready for breakfast.'

They went out of the yard to where the magnificent contraption had pulled up beside the pond, the four horses covered in lather. The general excitement was even greater than the day the Gotha crashed, the firemen swearing at the little boys that darted under their feet as they started unwinding the hose. Mark saw the man in charge, who glanced at the fire and the wind and the ricks and assured him that they would quickly have it under complete control.

'We can leave it to you, then?' Mark said.

'Certainly, sir. I take it you're the owner of this property?'

'I am. If you want me when you're through, I shall be up at the house.'

'Very well, sir.'

Mark turned and smiled at Christina. 'Breakfast, eh? What did you do with the horses?'

Christina hesitated. Urgently as she wanted to know about Dick, she saw that this was not the moment to turn away from Mark, who had done a magnificent morning's work. As if sensing where her thoughts lay, he said, less pleasantly, 'Come on, Christina. We'll go home. There's the little mystery of Tizzy to solve, if you remember.'

Christina shrugged and followed him across the ruts and puddles. The drizzle came cold and fresh across the first lines of plough. She slithered and stumbled, hardly knowing what she was doing.

'I let Pheasant loose. Can you see him?'

Hannibal had snapped his tether, but was grazing calmly on the verge. Mark caught him and led him up the track, holding Christina's arm, until they came across Pheasant eating the hawthorn hedge. Mark gave Christina a leg up, and then mounted Hannibal, and they rode up the track towards the covert side by side. Christina found that her legs felt shaky. After the wretched night she had spent, her thoughts were in a complete tangle. The only thing that occurred to her, and which made her smile involuntarily, was that she could scarcely keep her bold promise of going to live in the farm-house. But the bitterness of the night before had died. She did not know where she stood. She felt incapable of saying anything even remotely sensible.

'Had Tizzy been down to the farm, by the way?' Mark said. 'Before all the excitement?'

'Dick hadn't seen him.'

'We'll probably find him safe at home.'

'I expect so.'

A small, terrifying idea stirred in Christina's mind. It had come earlier, in the stable-yard, and been trampled in the ensuing events. She looked sideways at Mark.

'What do you think about the fire—how it started, I mean?'

'I think Dick was probably careless filling a lamp or something, and started it himself.'

Christina said nothing.

'He put up a damned good show getting it out, though,' Mark added.

'He said it had been started deliberately—'

'Oh, that's nonsense. As if anyone would! It was just a tale to cover up his own stupidity.'

Christina said nothing. She lifted her burning face to the damp, raw rain and prayed for the tangles in her life to get unknotted.

'It was a good fire,' Mark said. 'I saw the smoke from the windows when I got up. That's why I rode over. It was only rubbish that went, when all's said and done—although Dick was lucky to get the horses out. He's a good man in a tight corner, I'll say that for him; the sort of man I like to have in my platoon.'

'How extraordinary!' Christina thought. Everything she could think of was extraordinary. Mark had the expression on his face that she could remember seeing on it after a particularly good day's hunting: the satisfaction of a job well done, the pleasant, physical enjoyment of feeling tired for a good reason. He had enjoyed the fire.

As if he had sensed her thoughts he said, 'I've had enough of this leave. I'd like to get posted—with luck I shall go to France again.'

Christina shook her head, unable to say anything.

When they got back to the house Christina slipped upstairs, going in by the front door so as to avoid Mary. She went quietly into Tizzy's room. He lay in bed, his cheeks glowing with health. His eyes were shut, but opened abruptly when Christina stood over him. He looked at her, and she looked at his rain-damp hair, and the smut on his cheek. She saw the look of instinctive guilt flit across his face, to be blotted out by an enormous pretend yawn.

'Slept well, Tizzy?' she asked sweetly.

'Yes, oh yes. All night,' he said, gazing at her with innocent Russell eyes.

Tizzy, she thought, hadn't wanted to go and live in the farmhouse. Tizzy, a man of action like his father, had arranged things very well. He never thought to inquire after her own grotesque appearance, busy with his big pretend yawns, and rubbing his unsleepy eyes. Christina picked up his clothes, flung in a heap on the floor. They were damp, and smelt strongly of burnt straw.

'I think,' she said quietly, 'when Dr. Porter has seen you, you had better go and have a little talk with your father.'

He frowned.

'With who? Uncle Dick or Mark?'

'Mark.'

'What about?'

'I think you can guess.'

Tizzy sighed. 'I don' feel very well,' he said.

Christina, in spite of everything, laughed.

She went downstairs to fetch herself some hot water to get washed. As she crossed the hall the doorbell rang. She went and opened the door. A small elderly man in a black suit and a bowler hat, very neat and trim, looked at her, his mouth falling open as he took in her appearance.

'Mrs. Russell?' he faltered.

Christina's eyes fell on his brief-case.

'Mr. Perkins? Oh, please come in. We were expecting you.' She stood aside to let him pass into the hall, smiling sweetly through the soot. Inside she was saying to herself, 'Oh, heavens, whatever next?'

Chapter 13

An hour later, when Mark and Christina had washed and changed and breakfasted, they joined Mr. Perkins in the dining-room, taking their places solemnly at the big mahogany table. Christina, glancing across at Mark, was amused by the business-like face he was able to assume, in spite of swollen red eyes and a large sticking-plaster on his temple. His hands were gashed and blistered, fidgeting with the balance sheet Mr. Perkins had passed him for study. He scratched his head, swore and pushed his chair back, making for the decanter on the sideboard.

'I shall understand it better with a drop of lubricant,' he said plainly. 'A drink for you, sir?'

'Not when I'm working, thank you,' Mr. Perkins said, frowning.

Christina could smell the woodsmoke in her hair. She thought of Tizzy, and remembered the days when she had sat at this

151

table for dinner after hunting days, with Will and Mark and Uncle Russell. Mark poured himself a large whisky, and looked at the paper again.

'All these red figures,' he said. 'I take it they're debts?'

'That's right, Mr. Russell. I'm afraid it's not a very cheerful picture. Your father had raised a large mortgage on the house, and left a considerable number of debts, mainly to wine-merchants, horse-dealers, grain-merchants and that sort of thing—not very large ones individually, but, added together—er—' Mr. Perkins looked out over his half-moon glasses—'considerable.'

'You mean there's very little for me?'

'We have managed to settle most of the debts. Your biggest asset is the land and the farm-buildings, which you own. This house, I'm afraid, is in the hands of a financial company.'

Mark looked gloomily at the figures.

'That leaves me with just fields, then?'

'And the farm-buildings, as I said.'

'Well, we've just burned them down,' Mark said.

'Most unfortunate,' Mr. Perkins said formally. He paused, then said to Mark, 'I have been wondering if you are considering working the land? It seems to me that it is your only chance of making any money out of your property. I am talking of when the war is finished, of course, and you are released from your obligations in the military field.'

'The more I look at these figures, the more my obligations in the military field appeal to me,' Mark said gloomily.

'You think you might make the Army your career?'

'I'm not going to be a bloody farmer, if that's what you're suggesting.'

Mr. Perkins frowned again. Christina suppressed a smile.

'I'm afraid I must be plain, Mr. Russell,' the solicitor said. 'If you do not intend to earn any money by working, I cannot see any alternative other than putting the place up for sale.'

Mark glowered into his whisky glass.

'The old man left things in a fine pickle, I must say! I knew it was pretty bad, but—' He shrugged, shifting the papers about irritably. 'It's not as if I want very much: just a roof over my head and a hunter or two—'

'But you've no capital to live on, Mr. Russell,' Perkins insisted. 'If you were prepared to work—'

'What the hell can I do? I don't know the first thing about farming, or about anything else for that matter. The only thing I know how to do is hunt foxes and mount an attack on an enemy position. Both extraordinarily useless when it comes to making money. You had better put the place up for sale, then. And I'll go back to France and see if I can get myself killed.'

'Don't be so ridiculous!' Christina hissed at him across the table. 'You knew perfectly well how things stood! At least if you sold the place, you'd be able to keep a hunter at livery somewhere and enjoy yourself, wouldn't you?' His maudlin streak of self-pity annoyed her. Old Russell had cut Will out of his effects entirely, yet Will had worked sixteen hours a day seven days a week to earn the money to do what he wanted.

'Who would buy the old ruin, I'd like to know?' Mark shot back at her. 'At a time like this?'

'I would,' Christina said.

'Oh, you cunning b——!'

'Mr. Russell, please—' The solicitor's colour had risen and he looked uncomfortable, thinking privately that he had never come across a client who took more after his father than Mark Russell took after old Russell. Conferences at Flambards invariably ended in hard words; once old Russell had thrown a book at him. He looked at Christina, perfectly composed across the table.

'Are you serious, Mrs. Russell?'

'Of course she is. It's what she's been scheming for all along,' Mark said.

Christina, who had spoken the words the instant the possibility had entered her head, said coldly, 'You know perfectly well that the question has never been raised before. I wouldn't marry you in order to own Flambards, but I'm perfectly willing to buy it off you for its fair market value.'

Only the presence of Mr. Perkins stopped her from expressing her feelings about Mark's accusation more strongly. She felt slightly giddy by the turn the conference had taken, wondering if such a perfect solution to her future was indeed possible. In spite of Mark's suspicions, this particular solution had never entered her head before.

Mr. Perkins said cautiously, 'Your capital would, of course, easily contain the value of this estate, Mrs. Russell, if you think it would be a wise move from your own point of view—with regard to the future, I mean, and discounting sentiment—although, of course, it would be very satisfactory to keep the home within the family, I understand that . . .'

Mark pushed back his chair abruptly and said, 'Well, if that's the way of it, I don't see that my further presence is necessary. I take it I can trust you, Mr. Perkins, not to let this avaricious —, sorry, Mrs. Russell, swindle me? I'll stroll over and see if the fire that her employee started is now under control—'

'Mark.' Christina stood up (and Mr. Perkins put his head down, covering his eyes with his hand, with a little groan). 'Before you go, Mark, go upstairs and ask Tizzy about the fire. I think you'll find he knows how it started.'

'Tizzy?'

'Yes, Tizzy. *Your* son.'

Mark sent her a piercing glance. He picked up his empty glass and went over to the whisky bottle on the sideboard. 'Oh, my God,' he said. 'What a morning!'

Christina sat on, discussing her own financial affairs with Mr. Perkins, but conscious that her thoughts were elsewhere, concerned with Dick's health and Tizzy's fate upstairs as well as with the fantastic notion of herself being the owner of Flambards again. When Mr. Perkins seemed to have exhausted his figures she got up and suggested that she should go and make him a cup of tea, anxious to bring the session to an end. Once in the kitchen she had Mary's excitement over the fire to contend with. Fowler was sitting at the table with a mug of tea, all the latest details of the mopping-up operations at his finger-tips.

'Will you take a cup of tea in to Mr. Perkins, Mary?' Christina said sharply. 'Use the best china, and the silver tray. Has Dr. Porter been to see Tizzy yet?'

'No, ma'am. He's up in the village—you know Dick's been taken queer? It's the fire done it, of course—'

'Where is Dick? Where did they take him? What's wrong with him?' Christina turned on Mary, her voice shaking suddenly.

'They took him to Fowler's cottage, ma'am, and Mrs. Fowler took him in. They say he's been bringing up blood something awful, ma'am—' Mary's eyes shone with the glory of breaking bad news. Christina turned away, finding it impossible to say anything. Her strange and beautiful optimism, fired by Mr. Perkins, crumbled away, just as the stable walls had turned to ash against the clouds. She could not stand being stared at by Fowler and Mary, and went blindly out of the kitchen. She found she was shivering with *anger*. 'Not again! Not Dick!' She stood in the hall, her arms raised up, grasping the banisters, her face buried in the crook of her elbows. She heard Mr. Perkins cough in the dining-room, and turned and ran up the stairs. 'No, no—it's not true! The stupid, gloating, idiot old woman—it can't be . . .!' She hardly knew what she was doing, and stumbled over the frayed carpet.

'Ma!'

A pitiful small voice echoed down the landing. 'Ma, I want you!'

Tizzy stood at the door of his bedroom, all tousled and sobbing, his hands behind him, clutching his bottom.

'I hate him!' he sobbed. 'I hate him!'

'Tizzy!'

Christina went over and put her arms round the furious child, leading him back into the bedroom.

'Sit down! Don't be so silly!'

'I can't, I can't sit down—'

'Tizzy, stop it! You're a naughty boy, and you deserved it!'

'I didn't wan' to go away, Ma, an' I'm glad I did it, but I only meant to burn a li'l bit. Not all of it.' He hiccuped with tears. 'He beat me jus' like that man—'

'What man?'

'That man at—at—my dad did—like my dad beat me—'

Tizzy was evoking the memory of yet another father, Christina concluded, his father in Rotherhithe. She looked at the indignant eyes, the big tears rolling out in furious profusion, the lips trembling with mutiny.

'Oh, Tizzy, Tizzy!' He was hurt less by Mark's belt across his buttocks than by Mark's sudden reversal from soldier-hero to common, angry parent. Christina felt an unexpected pang of sympathy for Mark, who had received so many similar beatings from his own brutal old father that he had not paused to think of the relationship he was demolishing in his own first essay into violence.

'I'm sorry for you, Tizzy, but you deserved it, and Mark was bound to be angry. There, don't cry!'

She was torn between being stern and just and loving him desperately at that moment, because she wanted love and sympathy, too, in her own bleak situation, just as Tizzy wanted it. She pulled him on to her lap and he flung his arms round her, all damp and smoky.

'Oh, Ma, I don' wan' to go away ever—'

It was all her fault, perhaps, for giving him this sense of insecurity, of uprooting him in the first place. She remembered him standing on the stable roof when Dick had first come, and defying him with the same words. 'Oh, Dick,' she thought, clutching Tizzy—

'Dr. Porter's here, ma'am,' said Mary's voice at the door.

Horrified at the feeble, sentimental attitude she had been discovered in, Christina leapt to her feet, depositing Tizzy abruptly on to the floor. Dr. Porter came in, looking slightly surprised.

'Hullo, young man.'

Tizzy glowered.

Christina tried to explain. 'He's upset because he was very naughty and Mark's just given him a thrashing.'

'I wouldn't have thought he was in a fit state at the moment to receive corporal punishment,' Dr. Porter said stiffly.

Remembering that Tizzy had, in his unfit state, travelled out to the farm, set it on fire and travelled back again, Christina could hardly agree with the doctor's opinion, but she hadn't the energy to explain.

'He seems perfectly recovered from his fall.'

'Sit down, young fellow, let's have a look at you.'

While Dr. Porter examined Tizzy again, Christina found herself standing at the window where she had stood the evening before and watched Dick riding Pheasant in the dusk. It seemed days ago, not hours. She ached for Dick. She stood picking at a hole in the curtains. The park was bleak and empty, the drizzle still falling.

'No, there's certainly nothing to worry about there,' Dr. Porter said. 'He may as well get dressed.'

Christina turned round. Dr. Porter said, 'That was a bit of excitement up at the farm this morning! I thought—'

'Dr. Porter, how's Dick?'

'Dick?' The doctor was surprised by the urgency in Christina's voice.

'Mary said they'd taken him to Fowler's place and you'd seen him and he—he—she said he was—was vomiting blood—' Her voice dropped almost to a whisper.

Dr. Porter laughed. 'A spot, yes. Nothing to worry about, my dear. You know these village women—one drop of blood is three pints by the time the story's got around!'

Christina stared at him.

'You mean he's all right?'

'Yes, of course. I looked in, knowing his history, but there's no harm done. He'll have to rest for a few days, that's all.'

'Oh!' Christina felt as if the room was going round in circles. 'I—' She sat down on the bed. 'I thought I—oh dear!' If the doctor hadn't been there, she thought, she could easily have had hysterics. She wanted to laugh and cry at once. Dr. Porter looked at her closely. Then he came and sat down on the bed beside her.

'Dick has got a natural constitution like an ox, my dear, else he'd have died several times over before now. Having come so far, I think he's more likely to die of old age than anything else.'

Christina nodded. 'I love him,' she said.

'I see, my dear.'

They sat in sympathetic silence on the bed, and the model aeroplanes that hung from the ceiling on threads of white cotton revolved slowly in the draughts that whistled through the window-frame.

Tizzy, having hastily dressed, opened the door. 'I wan' my breakfas',' he said, and disappeared.

Chapter 14

'There,' Christina said, 'wasn't I right? Isn't he just the beast for you?'

Tizzy pulled the little Welsh pony to a halt by the gate and looked at her, pretending that he wasn't very impressed.

'For a little pony he's all right, I suppose.' But Christina could see the excitement in his face. He had cantered the pony all the way round the park, and the pony had gone eagerly, but without getting out of hand. Tizzy had been able to stop him without any trouble. Christina could see that he was proud and pleased, but did not want to show it. She laughed, stroking the pony's pinkish-grey neck.

'You're a good fellow, aren't you, Worm?'

'I'll ride him every day. I can take the beer out on him, can't I?'

'That's a good idea.'

'And you can ride that ol' Pheasan'. I don't like him very much.'

'He's nowhere near as well-mannered as Worm,' Christina agreed.

Away down the drive they heard the scrunch of hoofs on the gravel. Christina said to Tizzy, 'Mark is coming back. Don't dismount for a moment—wait and show him how well Worm goes for you.'

Mark had been away all day, having been summoned to London by the War Office. The telegram had come for him two days after Mr. Perkins's visit, and his eyes had lit up when he read it. He had whistled round the house, and stood over Christina while she pressed his uniform, and ridden Hannibal round the old point-to-point course out of sheer high spirits.

On his way to London he had ridden Hannibal to the station and left him in the stable of the Station Hotel, rather than be driven over by Fowler. Now, seeing him approach on the powerful chestnut, in uniform and looking every inch the cavalry officer, Christina felt her insides wince at the thought of his going back to the front. Their love-hate relationship had continued for so many years now, and their understanding of each other was so close, that it was no good pretending that she did not care what happened to him. She cared very much that he should be happy, which was why her own happiness in possessing Flambards and loving Dick was slightly clouded, impeded by a sense of guilt in gaining her desires at Mark's expense. Thinking this, she was frowning slightly as he reined up by the gate.

'Well, Christina, I've got my posting. I'm going to France on Friday.'

His voice was soft and excited.

'Oh, Mark! Is that what you wanted?' She tried to look pleased, not very successfully.

'Of course! It's splendid! My God, I was praying for it all the way up in the train. And another pip. What more could I ask?'

'Uncle Mark—Dad—I've galloped on Worm,' Tizzy called out. 'D'you want to see me?'

'I'll race you!' Mark called out, grinning. He swung Hannibal round and rode him into the park. Tizzy, his face alight with excitement, thumped Worm with his heels and shot away up the field. Christina, anxious and laughing at the same time, saw Mark, very careful not to let Hannibal overtake, pound away behind him, making loud hunting calls. At the same time, another noise, completely unexpected, caused her to swing round in surprise. A smart car was pulling up on the gravel.

'Whoever—' It was too late for visiting, the tang of evening frost already sharp on the dusk. Mary had lit the lamps, and the glow of firelight and lamplight through the long windows of the sitting-room, framed in ivy and the deserted swallows' nests, shone out across the drive. Christina, full of curiosity, went to greet the figure who was climbing out of the driving-seat. The figure turned round, pushing back scarves and veils.

Christina stopped dead, her hands flying up to her mouth.

'*Dorothy!*'

'Christina!'

They stood laughing, embracing, and laughing again, Dorothy clutching her hat, making excuses. 'I had to call in, although I've no time at all—you said Mark was here, and then I realized I hadn't seen you since—oh, for three years, surely? And I had your letter—'

'But you can stay? For tonight at least? You must!'

'Oh, yes, tonight I can, but tomorrow I—'

'Oh, Dorothy, I can't believe it!'

Christina heard the thud of hoofs coming towards them across the turf and Tizzy's laugh, a shriek of excitement. Worm pulled up, bobbing his head, and Hannibal skidded through the gate right behind him, spraying gravel, his breath making clouds as he snorted and curvetted, Mark pulling him in.

'Look who's here!' Christina called out. 'Mark, it's Dorothy!'

She saw Mark's head jerk round with astonishment, and Hannibal stood instantly, sensing Mark's change of mood. Dorothy went up to the big horse, reaching out to put a hand on his neck, but not laughing as she had laughed with Christina. Christina watched Mark's eyes run over her, full of pleasure and admiration. Dorothy had always been extremely attractive to men, but now, three years older and more experienced than when Christina had seen her last, she had a maturity which made her arresting. She was strikingly well dressed, even for driving, in a plum-coloured coat and an extravagant hat—the contrast in colour with her gorgeous auburn hair gave a slight shock: it was both surprising and absolutely right, with the considered attention to detail that had always made Dorothy a conspicuous figure. Christina, watching her, was conscious of her own untidy skirt and jacket, and the heavy coil of her hair pinned up with more regard for practicality than beauty.

The horses were put away, Tizzy introduced (Mark having the grace to flush slightly, and Christina talking to Tizzy about Worm so that he would not hear the necessary explanations) and they went into the house. Mary laid another place, excited by the presence of 'a proper lady', as she confided to Christina. Mark fetched out the best port and the crystal glasses. Dorothy played with Isobel, enchanted by the baby, and Tizzy rushed round as if he was still on Worm, until dispatched with water bottles to put in the spare bed. When the children were in bed, the three of them ate in the dining-room, and afterwards repaired to the sitting-room to talk. There was so much to tell, and Dorothy had to go in the morning—'Early, I'm afraid. This is the end of my leave—I'm going back to France on Friday.'

Christina glanced at Mark, and saw him smiling to himself.

'Where are you nursing?' he asked.

'At Etaples.'

'Obviously there are compensations for the wounded,' he murmured. 'As it happens, I'm going to France on Friday, too.'

Christina excused herself early, conscious that time was precious to Mark and Dorothy. Her thoughts were confused, with memories awakened by Dorothy mixed up with anxieties for Mark's future. But she slept soundly, in fact she overslept, and when she was at last awoken by Isobel's indignant cries she found that Dorothy had already gone, leaving a note of apology. Mark had gone with her.

'He said he'll be back tonight, ma'am,' Mary told her. 'Well, he'll have to be, to collect all his things, ready to go off. What a lovely young lady she is, ma'am, to be sure, a real town lady, not like the farmers' wives we get round here! I'm not surprised Mr. Mark wanted—'

'Yes, Mary. They were very good friends, you know, before the war started.' She did not want Mary to think that Mark could be infatuated quite so suddenly.

She was not sorry to be on her own. A sweet sense of freedom stole over her, like being a child again when dissenting elders were out of the way. After seeing to the children and tidying up and ordering lunch, and agreeing with Mary that they should try once more to find a girl to help in the house, Christina escaped outside. She did not want to do anything, only feel and think and look at things, aware that she had not done merely this for too long. 'I don't want to worry any more,' she thought. The morning was still and misty, the chestnut-trees a glory of wet gold leaves, the conkers fresh and shining in their split cases. Even the gravel smelt of earth, as if the earth beneath it was too strong to be muffled; the thick clay shone with moisture, the grass was still green, and the ivy on the house dripped and ran with the dew. Christina had time to take it all in, walking slowly away down the drive, kicking the stones.

She went to see Dick, walking, not in any hurry, for she felt that now the world was their own again. Mrs. Fowler, a little busy, fussing gnome, overwhelmed by Christina's appearance, never left her elbow from the moment she put her foot over the doorstep, so that communication with Dick was completely impossible. He sat in a chair on one side of the fire-place, and she sat on the other, and Mrs. Fowler talked. Christina sat looking at Dick, and he smiled at her, not embarrassed at all. Christina, strangely, found no reason to be put out, for she felt as close to Dick, under cover of Mrs. Fowler's voice, as if she were in his arms; in fact, it fitted in, the two of them restful and silent together, with her feelings of not having to worry. She did not have to ask him how he was, or where he was going to live, or if his chest hurt him, or whether he lost all his clothes in the fire; she had only to sit and look at him and think, 'I love him'— a great self-indulgence, a perfect luxury. He knew nothing of the upheavals at Flambards during the last two days, nothing of her quarrels with Mark, nothing of who was the owner of Flambards; she was unable to tell him, because of Mrs. Fowler, and found that it was quite unnecessary, and forgot it.

When it was time to go she thanked Mrs. Fowler, and got up. Dick got up, too, and Christina said the platitudinous things to him, about getting better quickly and not to be in a hurry to start work. She said them without thinking, and then looked at Dick, all her real thoughts in her eyes. She was very close to him, for the cottage was tiny and the chairs close together, and they put their arms round each other and kissed. Mrs. Fowler, for the first time, stopped talking. She never said another word, accompanying Christina to the door, her mouth wide open.

Christina ran home, leaping and bounding, as if she were a twelve-year-old. She thought of Mrs. Fowler, in bed with Fowler, telling him what she had seen, and laughed.

Mark did not get home until very late. Fowler went down to the station with the dog-cart, but Christina was already in her bedroom when she heard it return. She had not undressed, and was brushing out her hair. She heard Mark come upstairs. His footsteps came down the passage, and paused outside her door.

'Christina?'

She opened the door. He stood there, damp, slightly breathless, almost laughing. He came in and shut the door behind him.

'Christina, before I go—it's all right. I wanted to tell you.' He leaned on the door, his hands behind him on the knob.

'What's all right?'

'Everything. First, you having Flambards. That's all right. I'm not bothered now. I shall tell Perkins to go ahead and see that everything is put into your name.'

'Oh.'

Christina was more concerned for Mark than—at that moment—pleased about Flambards.

'You're—you're still going to France tomorrow?'

'Yes, of course!'

This, the reason for her sadness, was—amazingly—the prime ingredient of his happiness. He smiled at her, putting his hands on her shoulders.

'Listen, silly, everything has turned out marvellously—for me as well as for you. You don't have to look so worried. Dorothy and I are going to get married.'

'Oh!'

'And you will think me very cynical when I point out that Dorothy is very rich.'

Christina smiled suddenly. 'Richer than me?'

'Yes.'

'But you say you're still going to let me have Flambards? Surely if you—'

'No, we shan't live here. Not only is Dorothy rich, but she owns a house—a hotel—in Northamptonshire. She told me that when the war is finished she wants to make a living out of it— it's a seventeenth-century inn on Watling Street. Her father bought it as an investment. But—more to the point, Christina— it's in the most superb hunting country! The Pytchley and the Grafton—both on the doorstep—'

'Mark, did you know this when you proposed to her?' Christina's voice was stern.

'No, cross my heart, Christina! I got carried away. It seemed so stupid to dither about—there we are, both going to France together—and she made it pretty clear what she thought about me. She's obviously a more discerning girl than you, Christina. We'd had a marvellous day and—I must admit—I'd had quite a bit to drink, so I proposed to her. She *is* rather splendid, Christina, you must admit. And then, after we'd decided on getting married, it all came out about the hotel in her life. It's got six loose-boxes at the back—'

'Mark!' Christina was outraged, yet found she was laughing. 'Oh, Mark, she's my friend! You do love her—it's not just—just—'

'You are so earnest, Christina! Of course I love her. We'll get on famously!'

Christina, who knew the strength of Dorothy's will-power, as well as her temper, realized that in Dorothy Mark might well have met his match. They would love and quarrel passionately: they were both handsome, impetuous, arrogant, and self-willed.

'It could be a very good match,' she said, smiling. 'I'm very pleased!'

She was, too, which half surprised her. She had always felt slightly possessive of Mark when he had been interested in other girls, for no reason that she had ever been able to discover. But the thought of Dorothy as a sister-in-law was extremely satisfactory.

'Yes,' she said. 'You're very clever, Mark!'

He stopped looking excited suddenly, and said quietly, 'Not as clever as I might have been.'

'What do you mean by that?'

'Not as clever as either Will or Dick.'

Christina frowned, but Mark went on, 'I would rather marry you than anyone, Christina, even now. I shall never say this again, and I shall grow out of it, I suppose, but you might as well know the truth before I go.'

'We do nothing but quarrel, Mark. Always. We don't think the same way or want the same things. We never have.'

'I know.'

'Marriage would be terrible—you and me—'

'Yes, I know.'

'Well, then—' Gently. 'Just think about all the quarrels, nothing else. Everything is very well, the way it is. Don't spoil it.'

'No, I'm not going to. I just wanted you to know, that's all. It's the way you ride, Christina. I've never seen a woman who rides like you do. That's why I love you.'

Christina could not hide her utter astonishment. 'How extraordinary!' she thought. 'How like Mark! How utterly irrelevant!' It was the sort of remark she could start arguing with immediately. She laughed.

'Dorothy can ride. We went riding, once.'

'Well, she'll have to. Give me a kiss, Christina. Everything is different now. It won't be the same when we meet again. And don't worry about Dorothy—I'll make her a wonderful husband.'

They kissed good-bye. Christina was amused, but when she came to say something else, her voice was quavery. She opened the door for Mark.

'Just one thing,' she said. She cleared her throat. 'It's—it's Tizzy. You won't—'

'No. Tizzy is yours. I'll be an uncle to him in future. We've got two Russells between us, him and Isobel—Flambards' strain. You make Tizzy your heir, Christina, and I won't feel I've relinquished Flambards entirely. Dick can be his father.' He looked at Christina, a hint of the old mockery in his face.

But she was not to be baited now. 'Yes.'

'Good luck with your peasant!'

'Thank you. And good luck for you, too—in everything.'

When he had gone Christina undressed very slowly and got into bed. She did not feel like sleeping, but stared up at the cracks on the ceiling, thinking to herself: 'How extraordinary!' Life was extraordinary, throwing up suprises all the way. She reflected on all the things that had happened, her eyes tracing the cracks in the moonlight, and the things that were going to happen; she heard Isobel stir in her cot, and the barn-owl shrieking in the covert. She felt the house solid around her, unperturbed through eighty years of tiny human crises: births, deaths, and passions; she smelt the October frost on the windowpane. She remembered Will, and thought of Dick. Marigold padded past her door along the landing, on her way from Tizzy's encircling arm to the puppies that waited for her in the kitchen. As she lolloped down the stairs the grandfather clock in the hall struck eleven.

Christina was very much aware that nothing was really resolved, life's surprises were by no means finished.

'But the omens are good,' she said, and smiled at the ceiling. She was content.

Also in this series

The Eagle of the Ninth
Rosemary Sutcliff

ISBN 0 19 271765 0

The Ninth Legion marched into the mists of northern Britain. And they never came back. Four thousand men disappeared and the Eagle standard was lost. Marcus Aquila, a young Roman officer, needs to find out what happened to his father and the Ninth Legion. He sets out into the unknown territory of the north on a quest so hazardous that no one expects him to return . . .

Outcast
Rosemary Sutcliff

ISBN 0 19 271766 9

Sickness and death came to the tribe. They said it was because of Beric, because he had brought down the Anger of the Gods. The warriors of the tribe cast him out. Alone without friends, family or tribe, Beric faces the dangers of the Roman world.

The Silver Branch
Rosemary Sutcliff

ISBN 0 19 271765 2

Violence and intrigue are undermining Rome's influence in Britain. And in the middle of the unrest, Justin and Flavius uncover a plot to overthrow the Emperor. In fear for their lives, they find themselves leading a tattered band of loyalists into the thick of battle in defence of the honour of Rome.

The Lantern Bearers
Rosemary Sutcliff
Winner of the Carnegie Medal

ISBN 0 19 271763 4

The last of the Roman army have set sail and left Britain for ever. They have abandoned the country to civil war and the threat of Saxon invasion. When his home and all he loves are destroyed, Aquila fights to bring some meaning back into his life, and with it the hope of revenge . . .

The Ship That Flew
Hilda Lewis

ISBN 0 19 271768 5

Peter sees the model ship in the shop window and he wants it more than anything else on earth. But it is no ordinary model. The ship takes Peter and his brother and sisters on magical flights, wherever they ask to go. They fly around the world and back into the past. But how long can you keep a ship that is worth everything in the world, and a bit over . . . ?

Minnow on the Say
Philippa Pearce

ISBN 0 19 271778 2

David couldn't believe his eyes. Wedged by the landing stage at the bottom of the garden was a canoe. The *Minnow*. David traces the canoe's owner, Adam, and they begin a summer of adventures. The *Minnow* takes them on a treasure hunt along the river. But they are not the only people looking for treasure, and soon they are caught in a race against time . . .

Tom's Midnight Garden
Philippa Pearce
Winner of the Carnegie Medal

ISBN 0 19 271793 6 (hardback)
ISBN 0 19 271777 4 (paperback)

Tom has to spend the summer at his aunt's and it seems as if nothing good will ever happen again. Then he hears the grandfather clock strike thirteen—and everything changes. Outside the door is a garden—a garden that shouldn't exist. Are the children there ghosts—or is it Tom who is the ghost?

A Little Lower than the Angels
Geraldine McCaughrean
Winner of the Whitbread Children's Novel Award

ISBN 0 19 271780 4

Gabriel has no idea what the future will hold when he runs away from his apprenticeship with the bad-tempered stonemason. But God Himself, in the shape of playmaster Garvey, has plans for him. He wants Gabriel for his angel . . . But will Gabriel's new life with the travelling players be any more secure? In a world of illusion, people are not always what they seem. Least of all Gabriel.

Brother in the Land
Robert Swindells

ISBN 0 19 271785 5

Danny's life will never be the same again. He is one of the unlucky ones. A survivor. One of those who have come through a nuclear holocaust alive. He records the sights and events around him, all the time struggling to keep himself and his brother alive.

A Pack of Lies
Geraldine McCaughrean
Winner of the Carnegie Medal and
the Guardian Children's Fiction Award

ISBN 0 19 271788 X

Ailsa's life is turned upside down when a strange man moves into her mother's antique shop. He keeps the customers spellbound with his out-rageous stories—adventure, horror, romance, mystery—but Ailsa doesn't believe a word. It's all just a pack of lies . . .

Flambards
K. M. Peyton

ISBN 0 19 271783 9

Twelve-year-old Christina is sent to live in a decaying old mansion with her fierce uncle and his two sons. She soon discovers a passion for horses and riding, but she has become part of a strange family. This brooding household is divided by emotional undercurrents and cruelty . . .

This is the first book in the award-winning Flambards series.

The Edge of the Cloud
K. M. Peyton
Winner of the Carnegie Medal

ISBN 0 19 271782 0

Christina and Will have run away together, leaving the tense atmosphere of Flambards behind. Will is determined to fly one of the new aeroplanes that are all the rage now, in the early years of the twentieth century. Meanwhile, Christina finds that people frown on a young girl working for a living. And worst of all, Christina realizes that with Will, she will always come second to his passion for machines.

This is the second book in the Flambards series.

Flambards Divided
K. M. Peyton

ISBN 0 19 271787 1

The old ivy-covered house of Flambards has seen many changes since Christina first arrived as a girl of twelve. With the First World War coming to an end, Christina feels the time has come to leave the past behind and look to the future with Dick, the former groom in the stables. But the local gentry refuse to accept Dick into their society and when Major Mark Russell returns from the war in France, Christina finds her feelings divided between these two very different men in her life.

This is the final book in the Flambards series.

Wolf
Gillian Cross
Winner of the Carnegie Medal

ISBN 0 19 271784 7

Cassy hears sinister footsteps in the middle of the night. Suddenly she is packed off to stay with her beautiful, feckless mother. There is no explanation. Something has gone frighteningly wrong.

Danger is coming after Cassy. And behind it lurks the dark wolf-shape that seems to slink into everything.

Even her dreams.

The Great Elephant Chase
Gillian Cross
Winner of The Smarties Prize and the Whitbread Children's Novel Award

ISBN 0 19 271786 3

The elephant changed their lives for ever. Because of the elephant, Tad and Cissie become entangled in a chase across America, by train, by flatboat and steam boat. Close behind is Hannibal Jackson, who is determined to have the elephant for himself. And how do you hide an enormous Indian elephant?

The Hounds of the Morrigan
Pat O'Shea

ISBN 0 19 271773 1

The Great Queen, the Morrigan, is coming from the West, bringing destruction to the world. Only two children can stop her. At times their task seems impossible, and danger is always present. But they are guided in their quest by an unforgettable collection of humorous and joyful characters.

But all the time the Morrigan's hounds are trailing them . . .

The Gauntlet
Ronald Welch

ISBN 0 19 271762 6

Stumbling upon the old gauntlet is just the start of an amazing adventure for Peter. Suddenly he finds himself in the fourteenth century, in a world of castles, feasts and battles, where death and danger are always around the corner. Peter quickly learns to hawk, shoot a longbow, and fight with the best of them, before facing up to his biggest challenge. Can Peter escape from the besieged castle and return to his own time, or will he be another casualty of war himself?